W9-CME-663

Hi, Parents!

Your child's love of reading starts here, with HarperAlley's **I Can Read Comics**!

HARPER alley

**I Can Read Comics** introduces children to the world of graphic novel storytelling and encourages visual literacy in emerging readers. Comics inspire reader engagement unlike any other format. They ask readers to infer and answer questions, like:

1. What do I read first? Image or text?
2. Why is this word balloon shaped this way, and that word balloon shaped that way?
3. Why is a character making that facial expression? Are they happy, angry, excited, sad?

From the comics your child reads with you to the first comic they read on their own, there are **I Can Read Comics** for every stage of reading:

LEVEL 1

Simple stories for shared reading.

LEVEL 2

Engaging stories for children reading on their own.

LEVEL 3

Complex stories for independent readers.

The magic of graphic novel storytelling lies between the gutters.
Unlock the magic with…

# I Can Read Comics!

Visit **ICanRead.com** for information on enriching your child's reading experience.

# I Can Read *Comics* Cartooning Basics

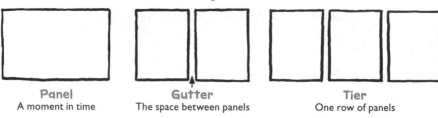

**Panel**
A moment in time

**Gutter**
The space between panels

**Tier**
One row of panels

**Word Balloons**  When someone talks, thinks, whispers, or screams, their words go in here:

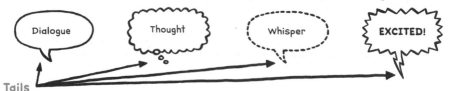

Dialogue

Thought

Whisper

EXCITED!

**Tails**
Point to whoever is talking / thinking / whispering / screaming / etc.

## A quick how-to-read comics guide:

In a **panel**, read the text on the **left** first.

Then, read the text on the **right**.

On a page, **start here**, in the **top left** corner!

After that, read the panel immediately to the **right**.

When you're done up there, come down here and read **this** panel **next**!

ME NEXT!
ME NEXT!

You're almost there...

**YOU MADE IT!**
You just read a comic page!

YAY!

## Remember to...

Read the text along with the image, paying close attention to the character's acting, the action, and/or the scene. Every little detail matters!

### No dialogue? No problem!

If there is no dialogue within a panel, take the time to read the image. Visual cues are just as important as text, so don't forget about them!

HarperAlley is an imprint of HarperCollins Publishers.
I Can Read® and I Can Read Book® are trademarks of HarperCollins Publishers.

Baby Shark's Big Show!: The Bunny Slug
© The Pinkfong Company. All Rights Reserved. Pinkfong™ Baby Shark™ and Baby Shark's Big Show!™ are trademarks of The Pinkfong Company, registered or pending rights worldwide. © 2022 Viacom International Inc. All Rights Reserved. Nickelodeon is a trademark of Viacom International Inc.
Printed in the United States of America.

Library of Congress Control Number: 2021951493
ISBN 978-0-06-315893-1

Book design by Elaine Lopez-Levine
22 23 24 25 26  LBM  10 9 8 7 6 5 4 3 2 1  ❖  First Edition

# I Can Read! Comics
**LEVEL 1**

BABY SHARK'S BIG SHOW!
pinkfong

# The Bunny Slug

STEVE FOXE   JASON FRUCHTER

HARPER alley

An Imprint of HarperCollinsPublishers

nickelodeon

One fine day under the sea, Grandma Shark was teaching Baby Shark and William how to meditate.

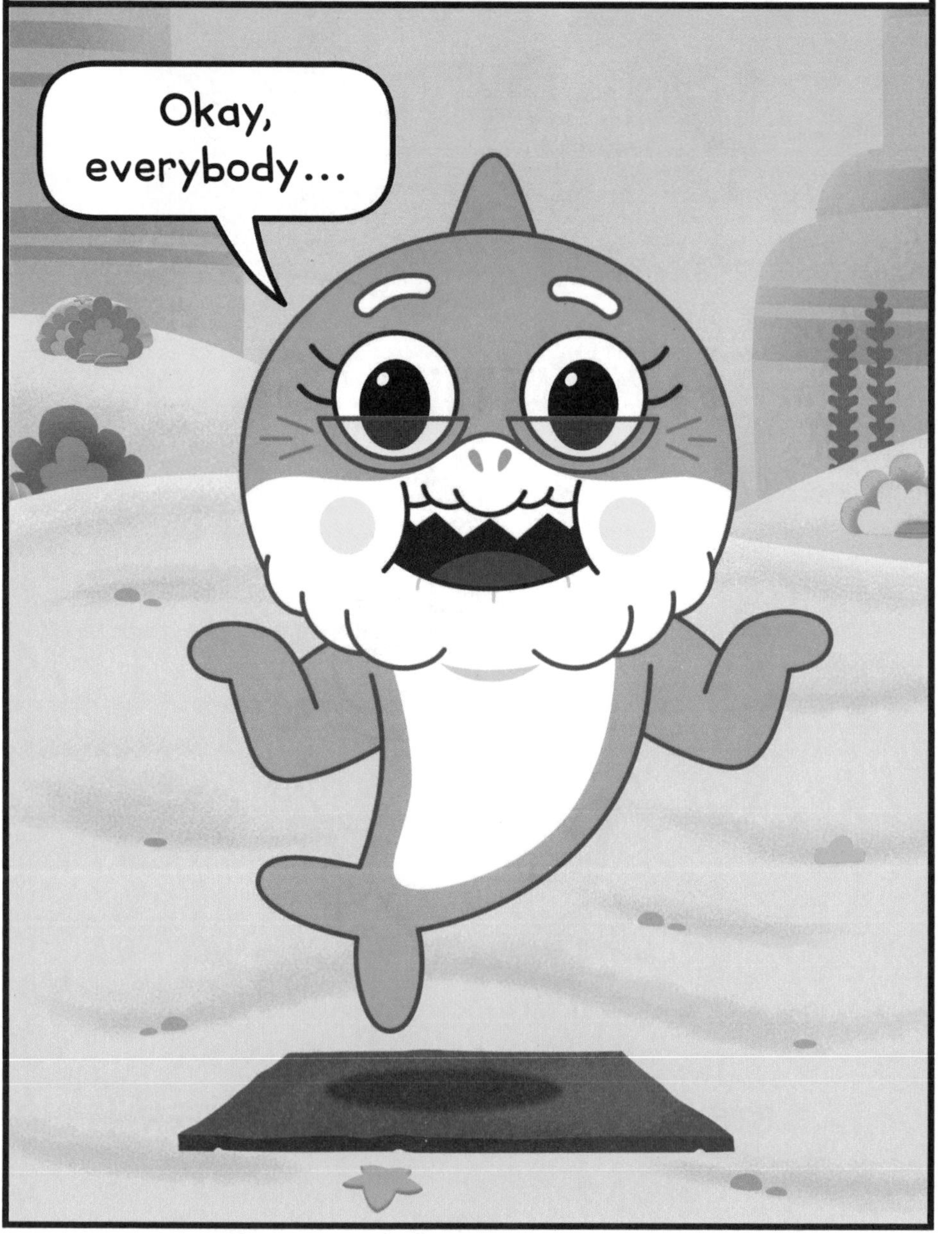
Okay, everybody...

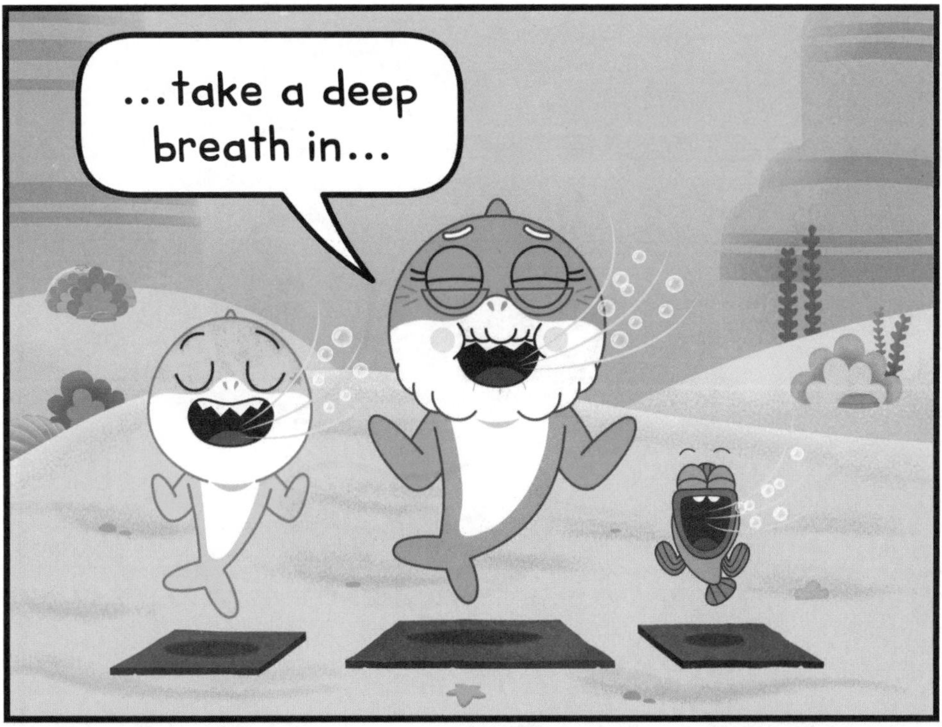
...take a deep breath in...

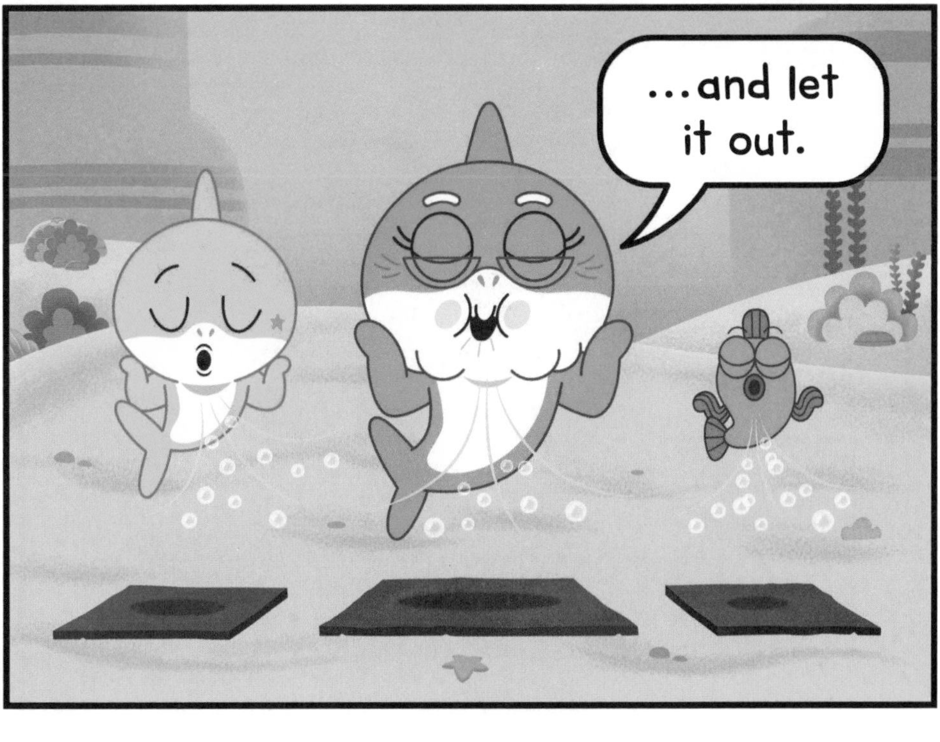
...and let it out.

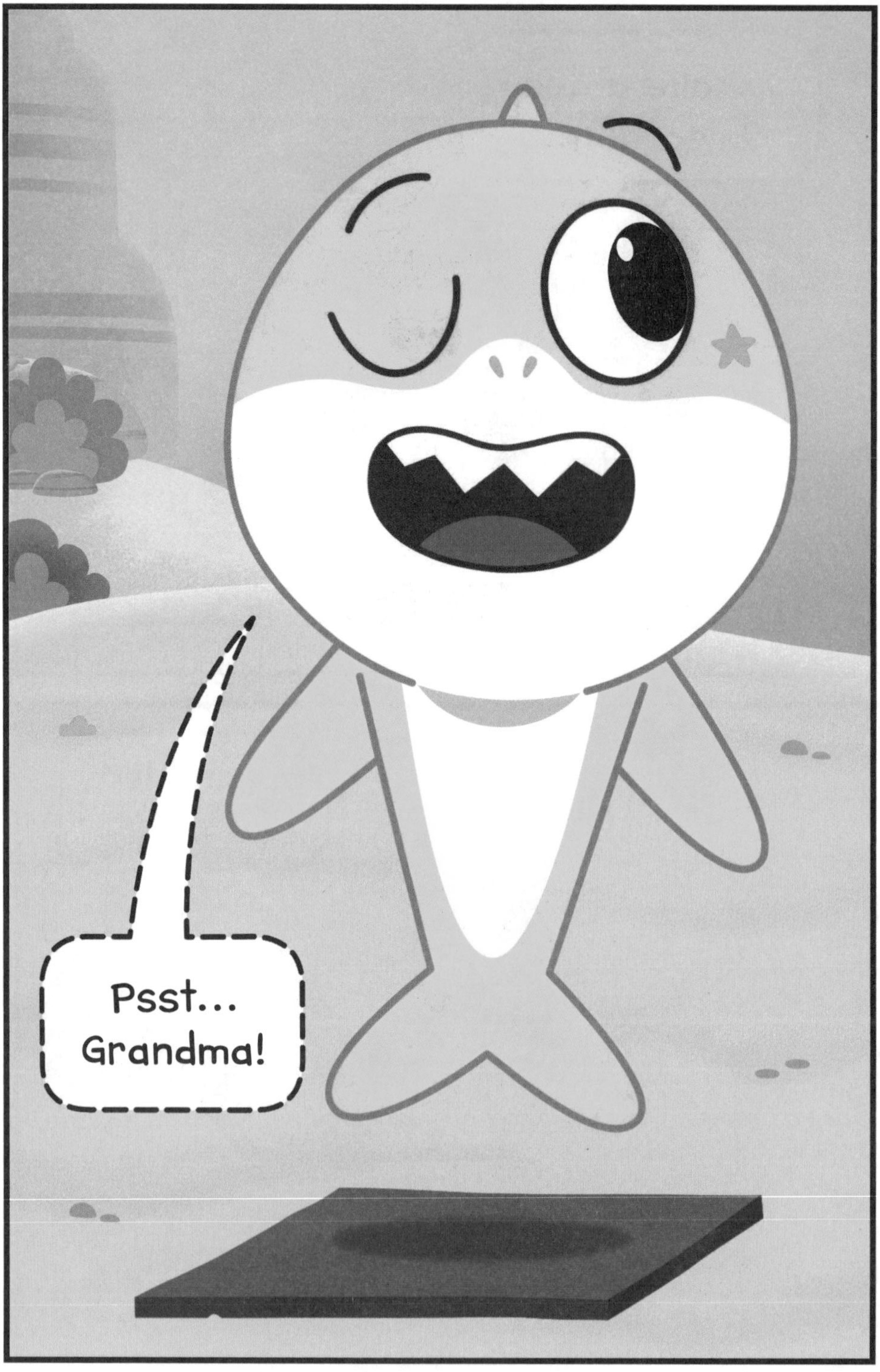
Psst... Grandma!

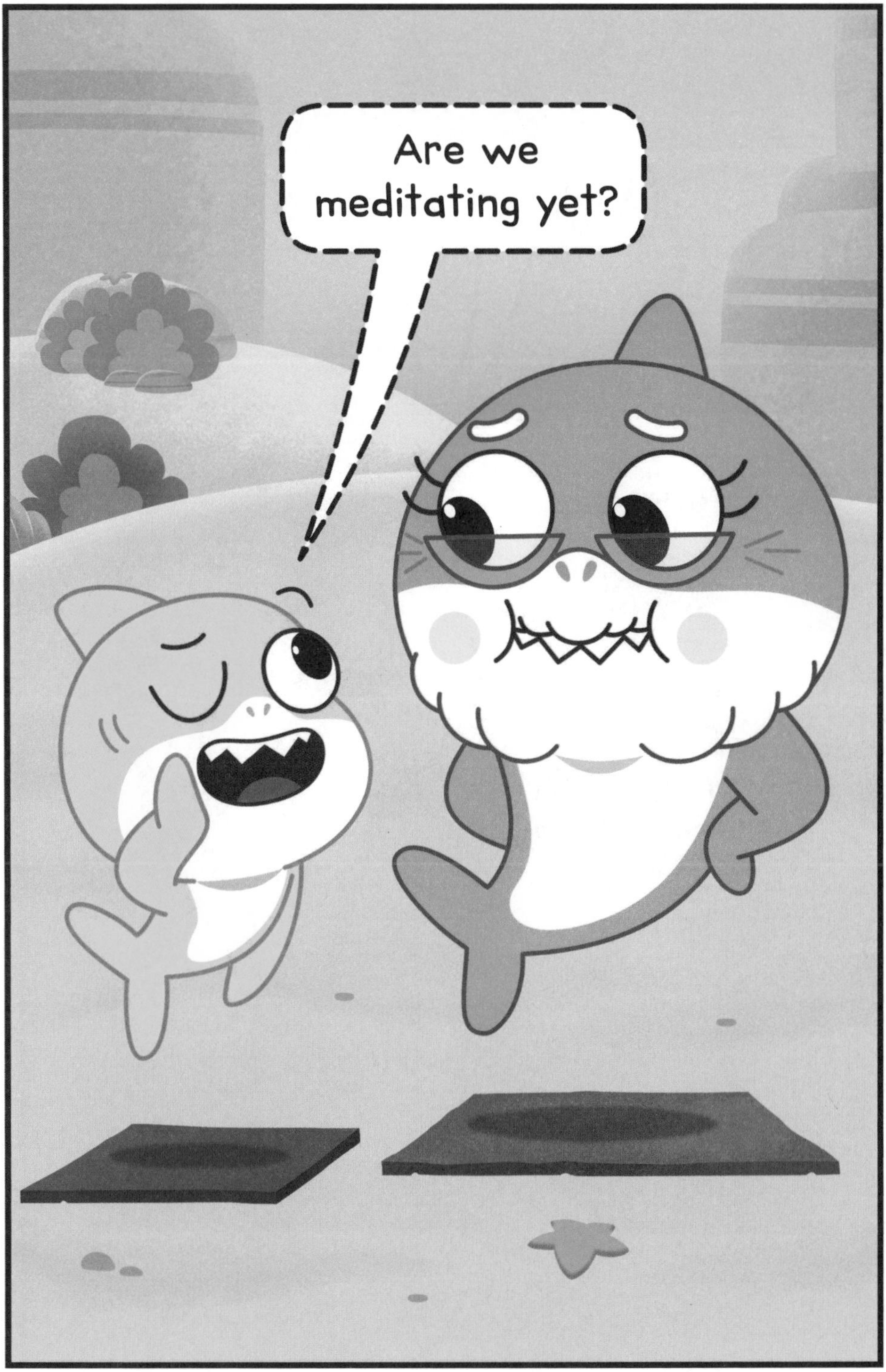
Are we meditating yet?

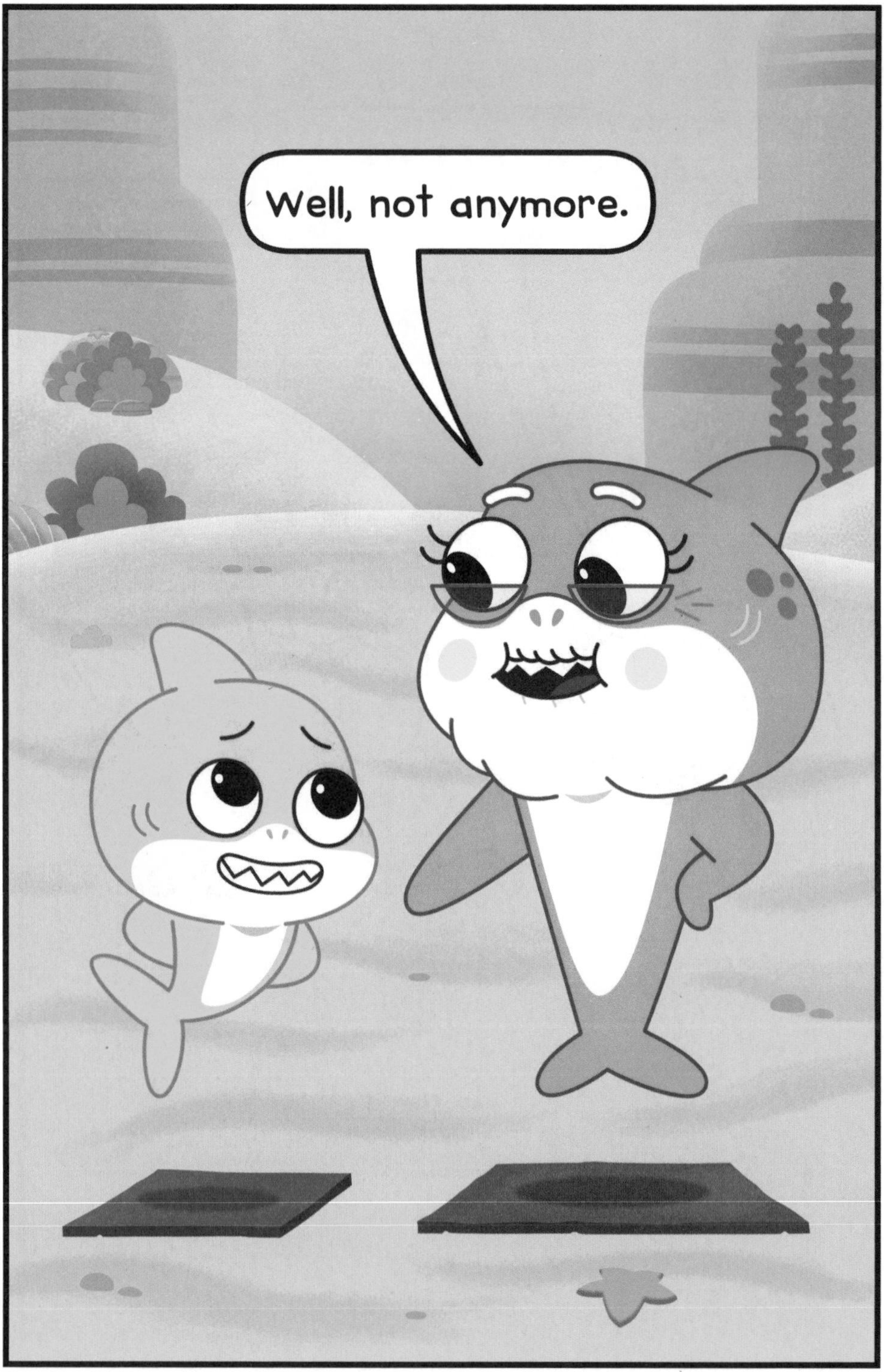
Well, not anymore.

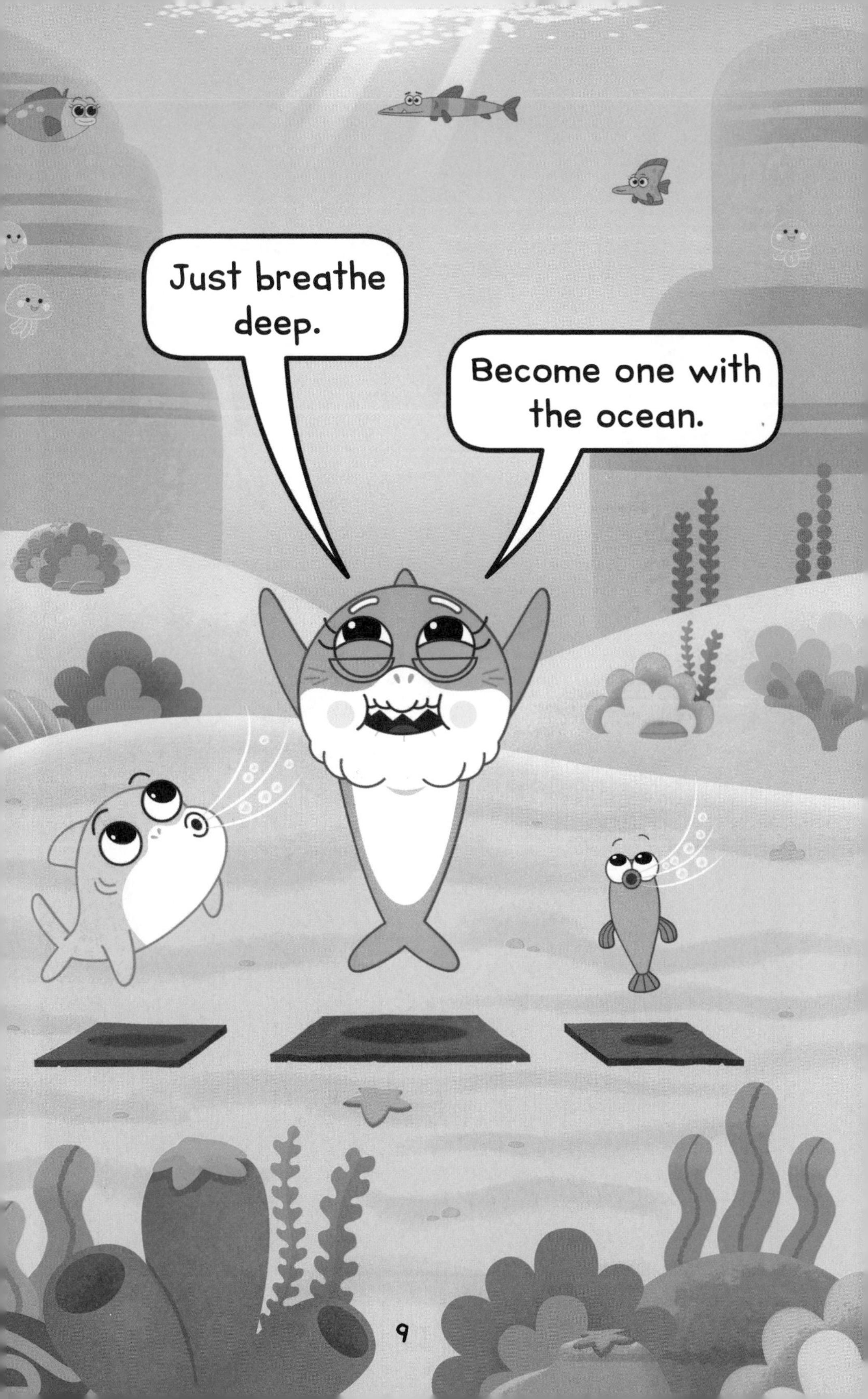
Just breathe deep.
Become one with the ocean.

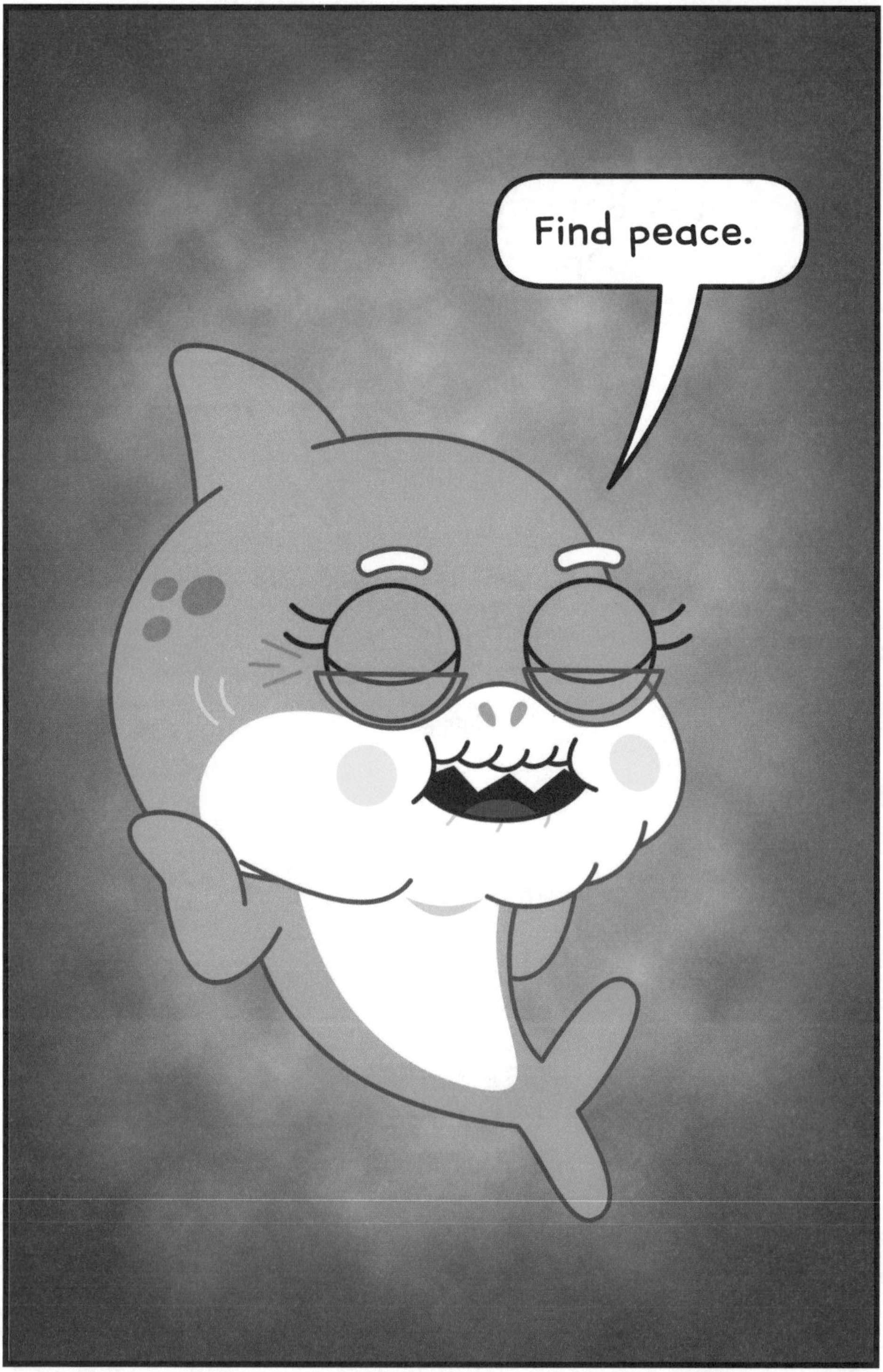
Find peace.

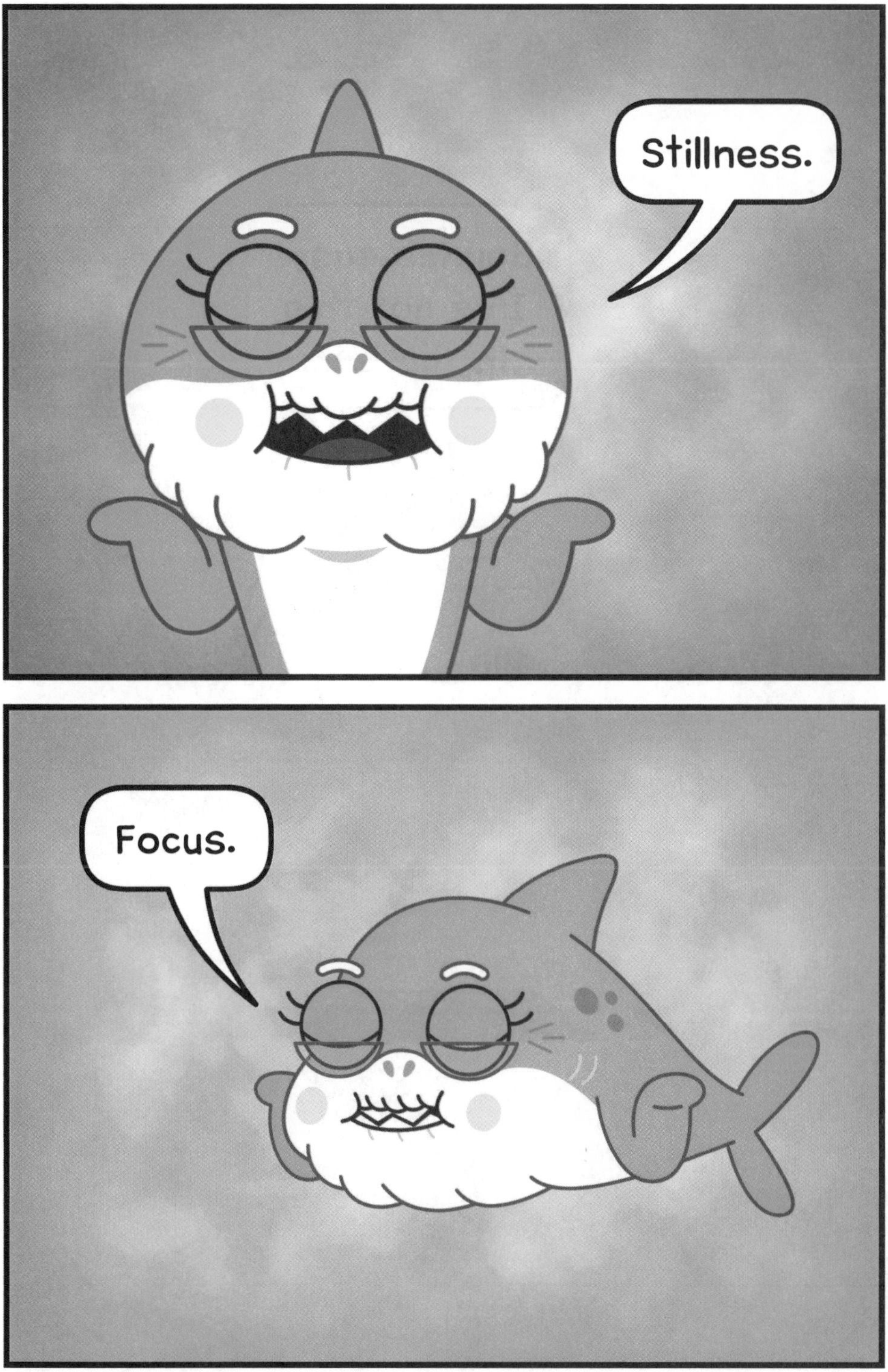
Stillness.
Focus.

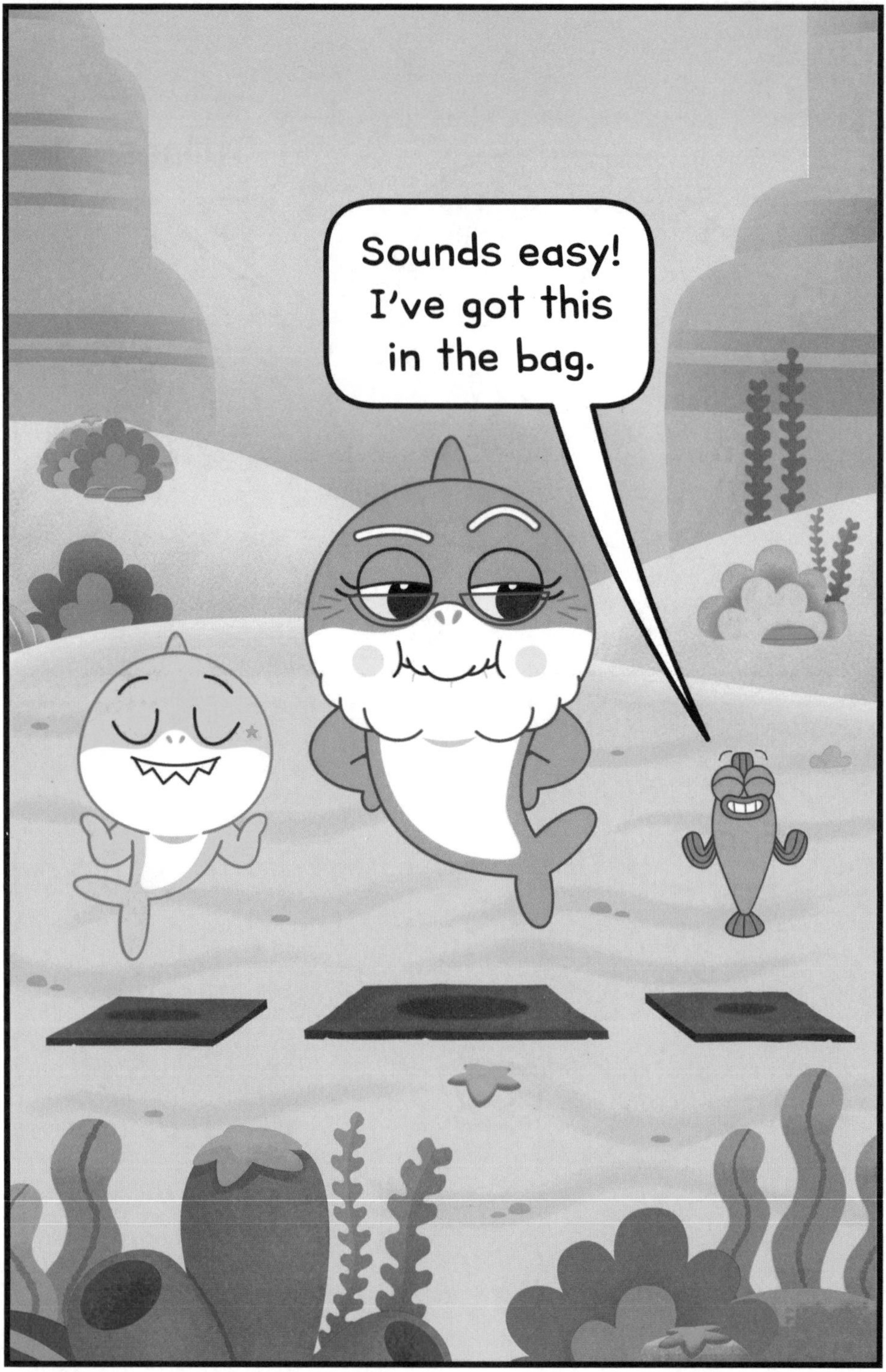
Sounds easy! I've got this in the bag.

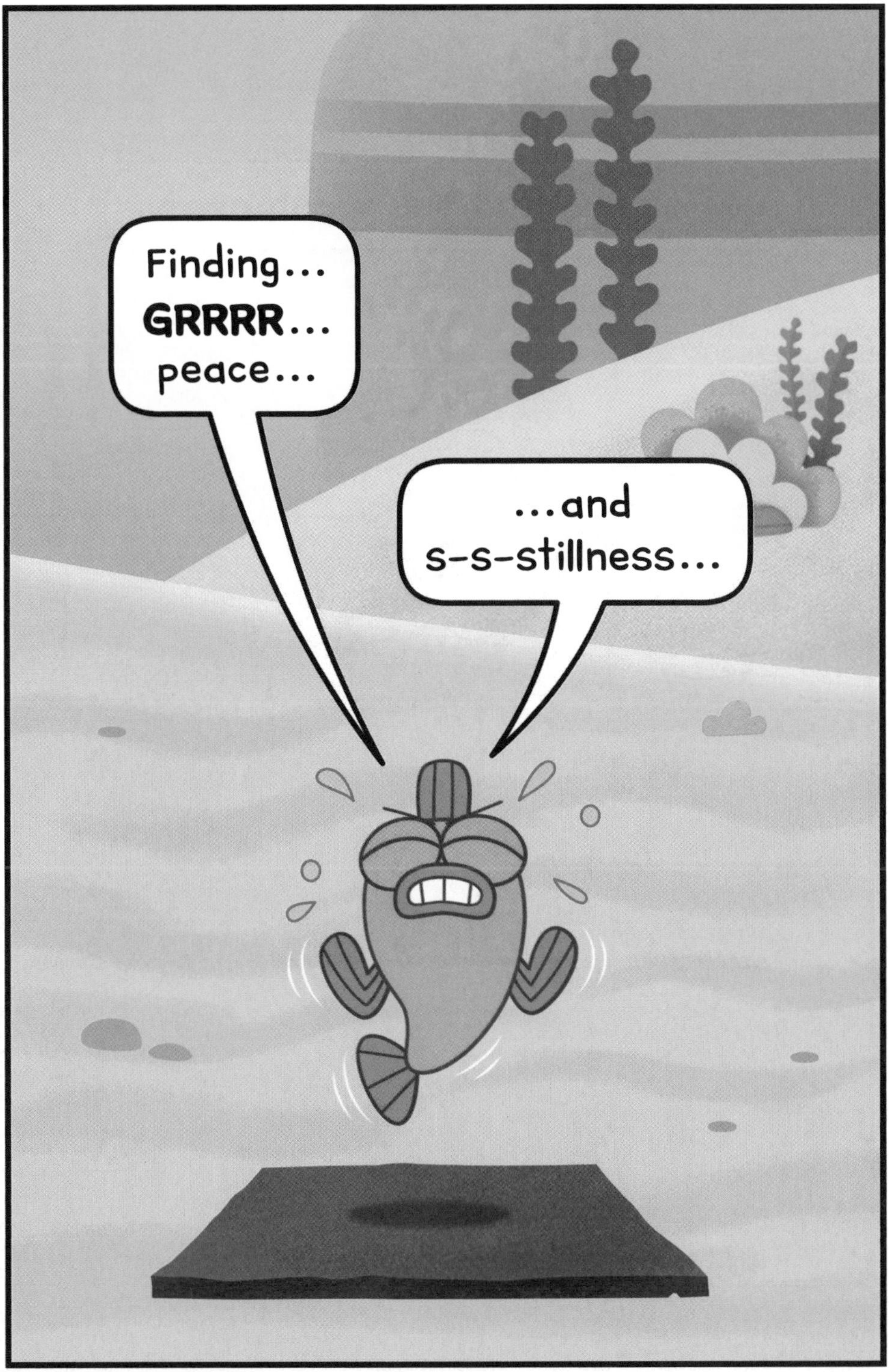
Finding... **GRRRR**... peace...
...and s-s-stillness...

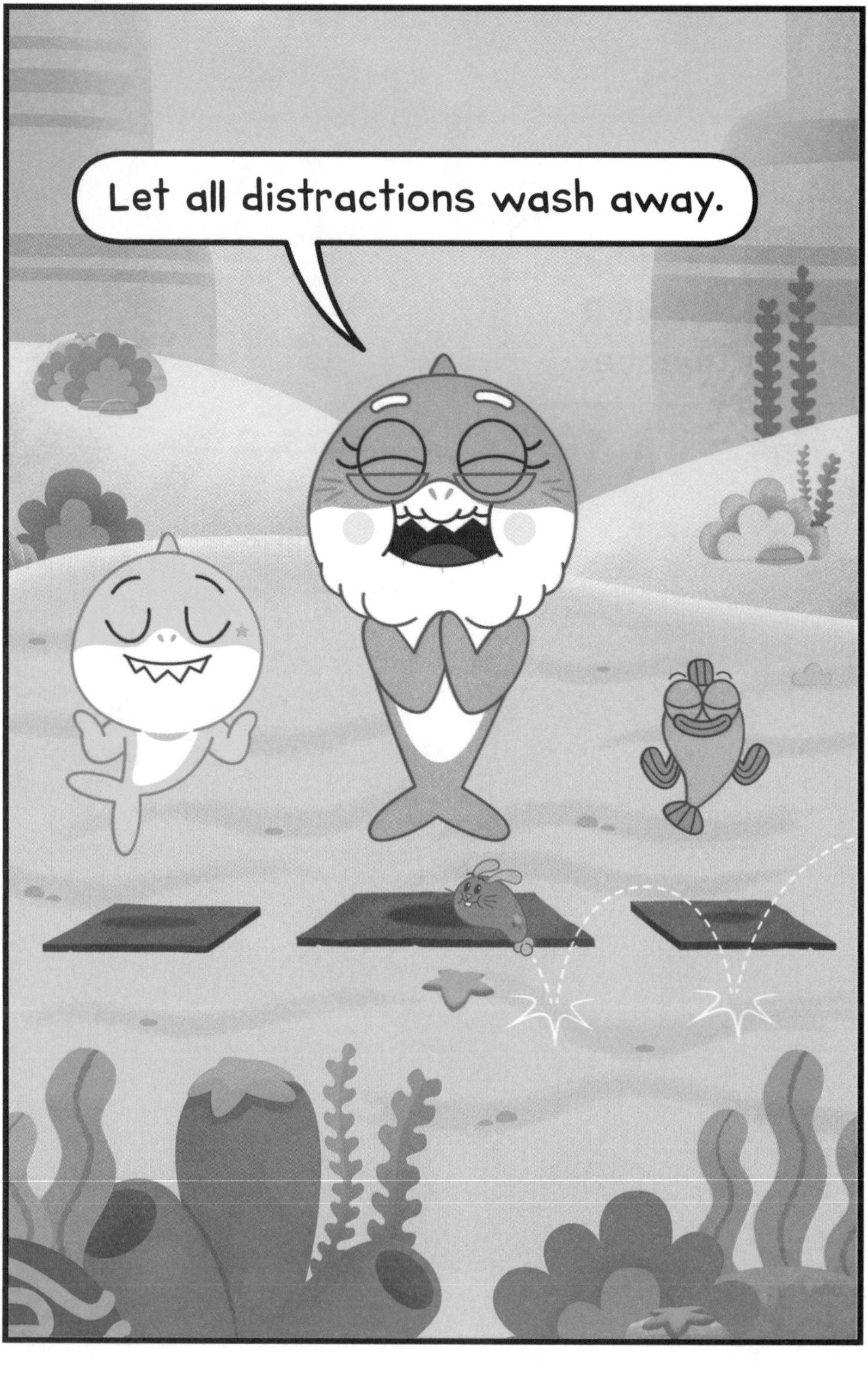
Let all distractions wash away.

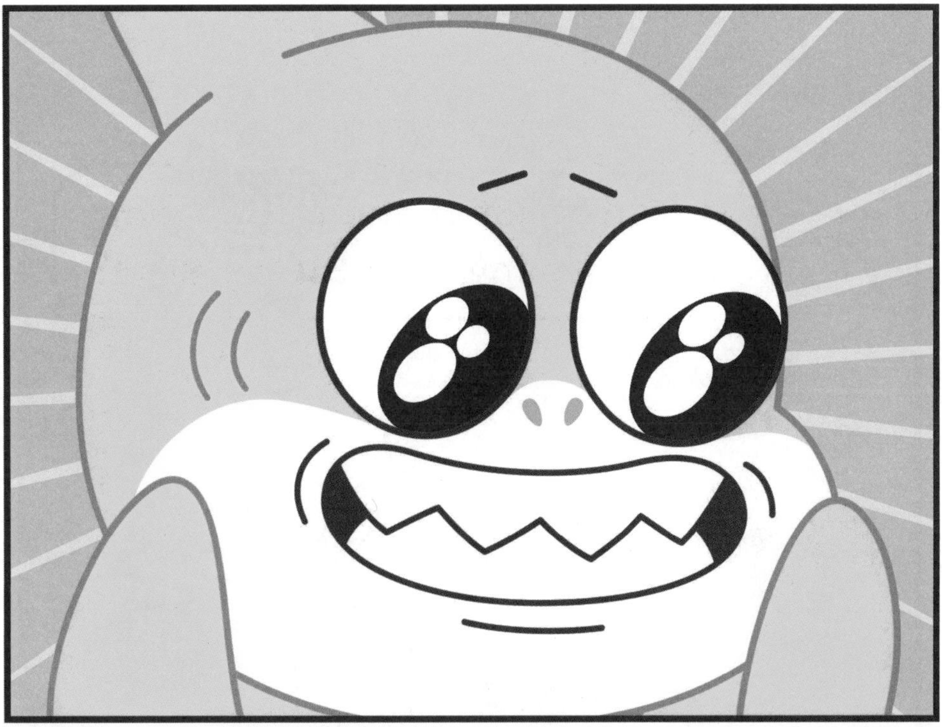

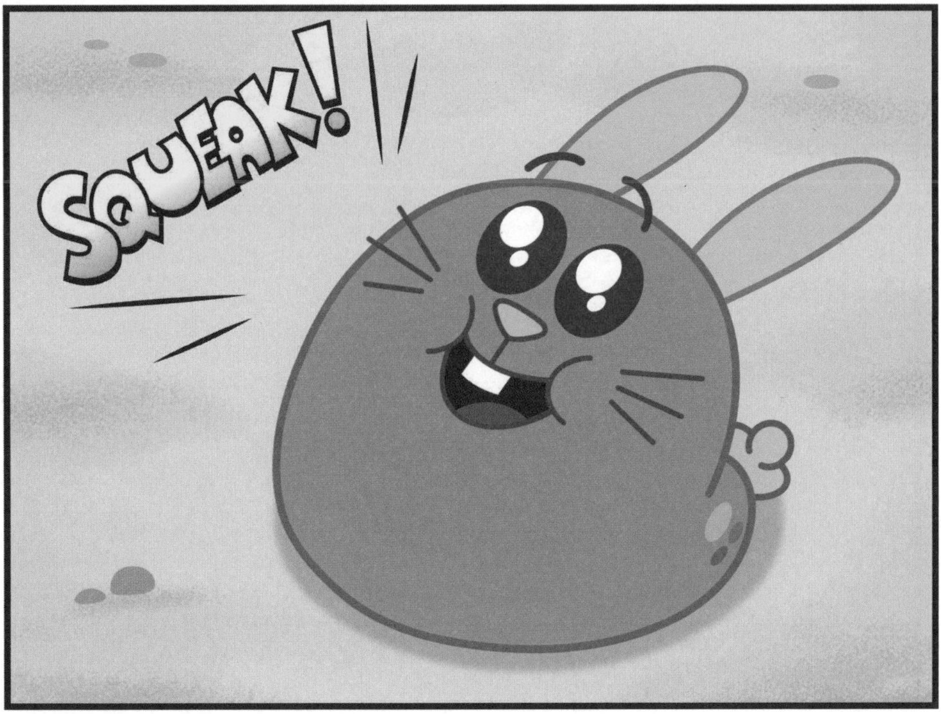
SQUEAK!

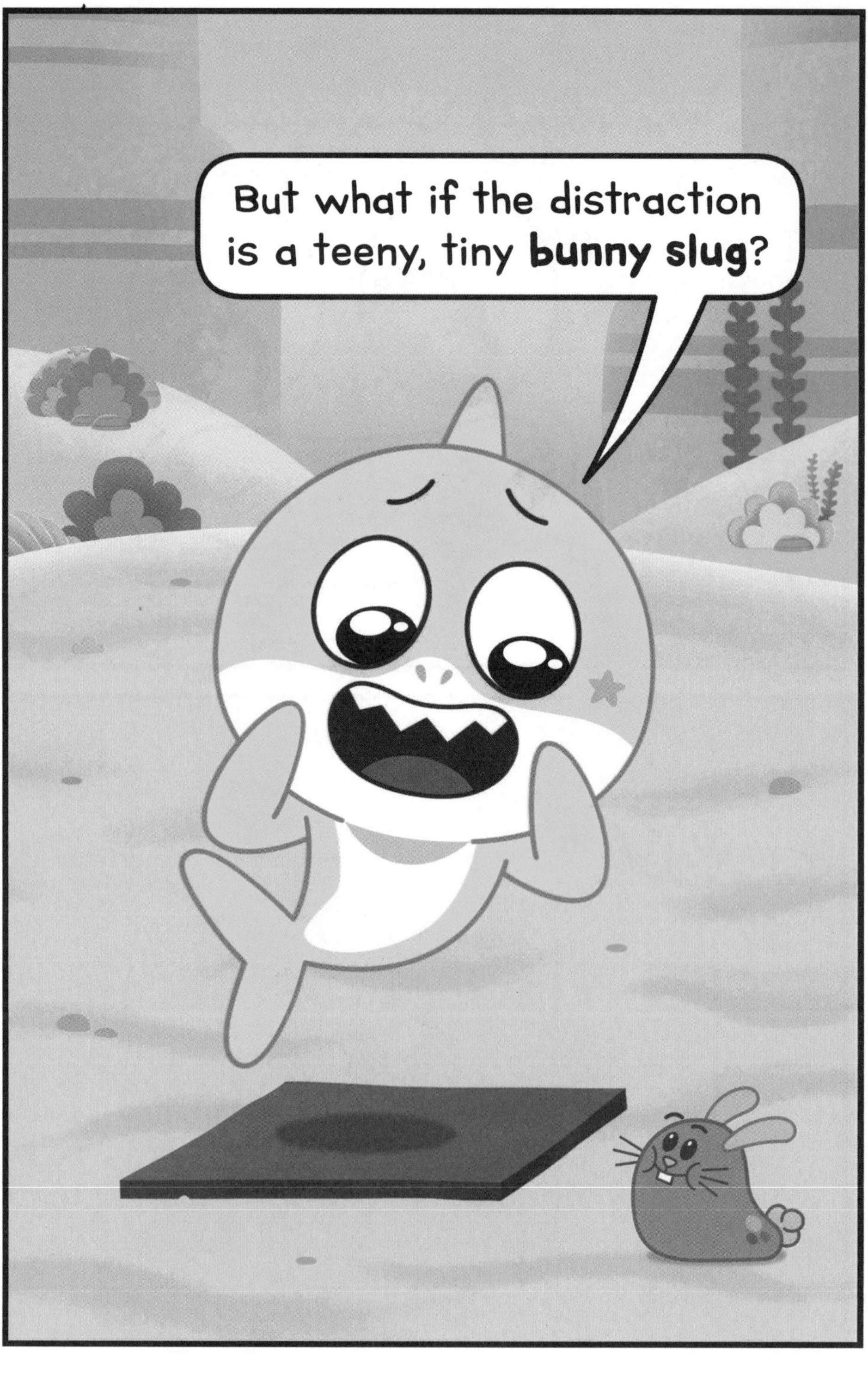
But what if the distraction is a teeny, tiny **bunny slug**?

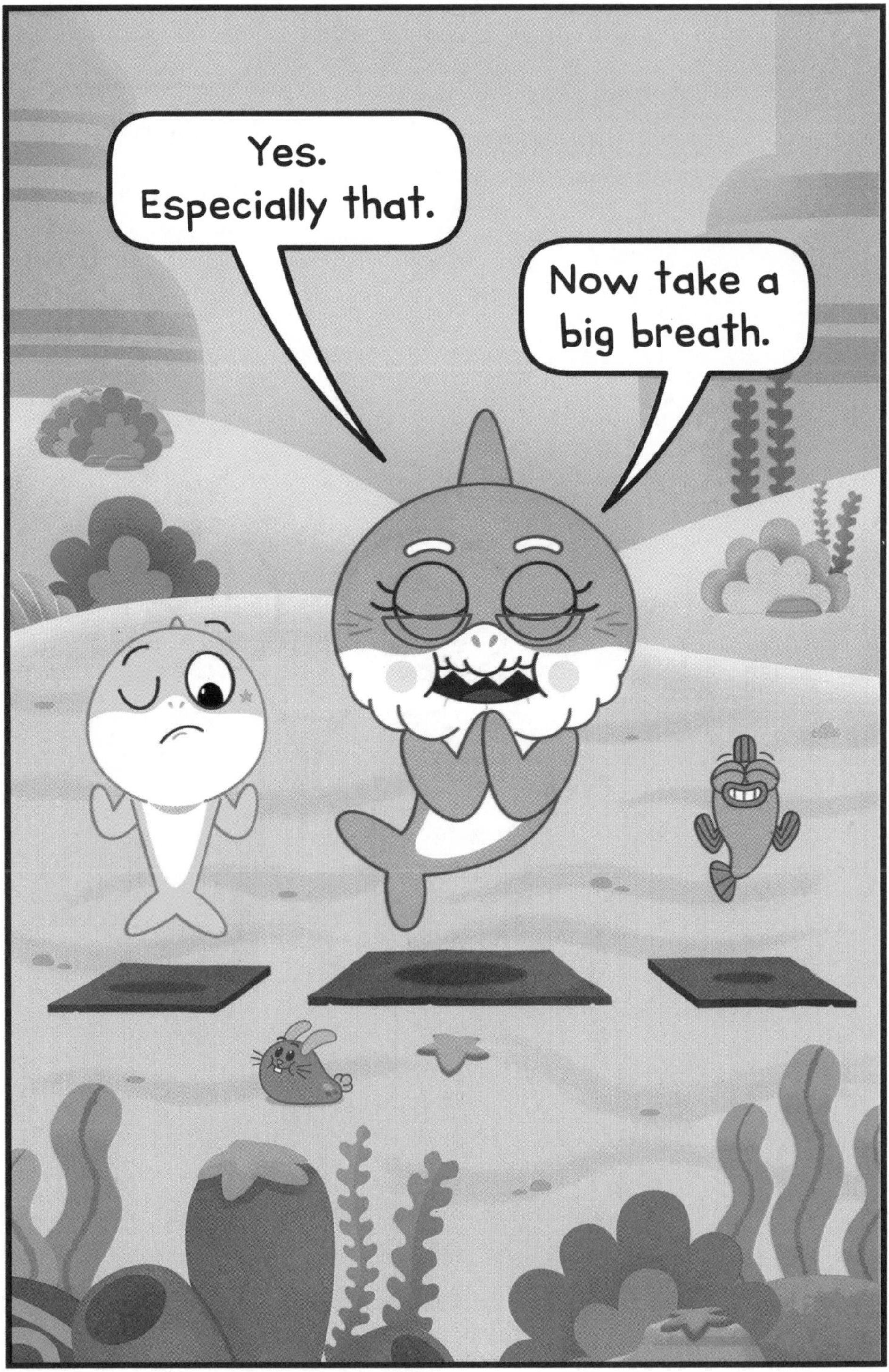
Yes.
Especially that.
Now take a
big breath.

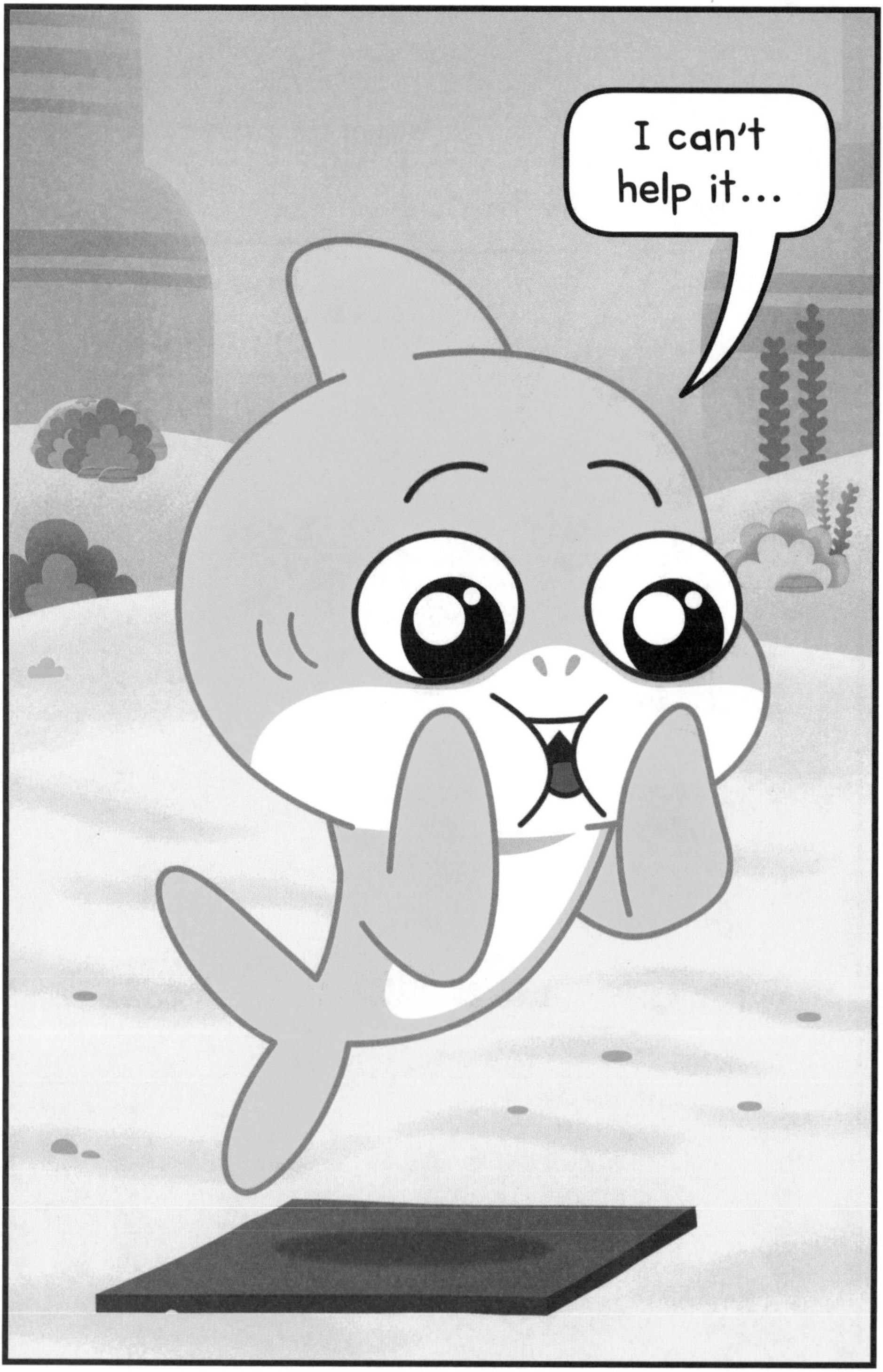
I can't help it...

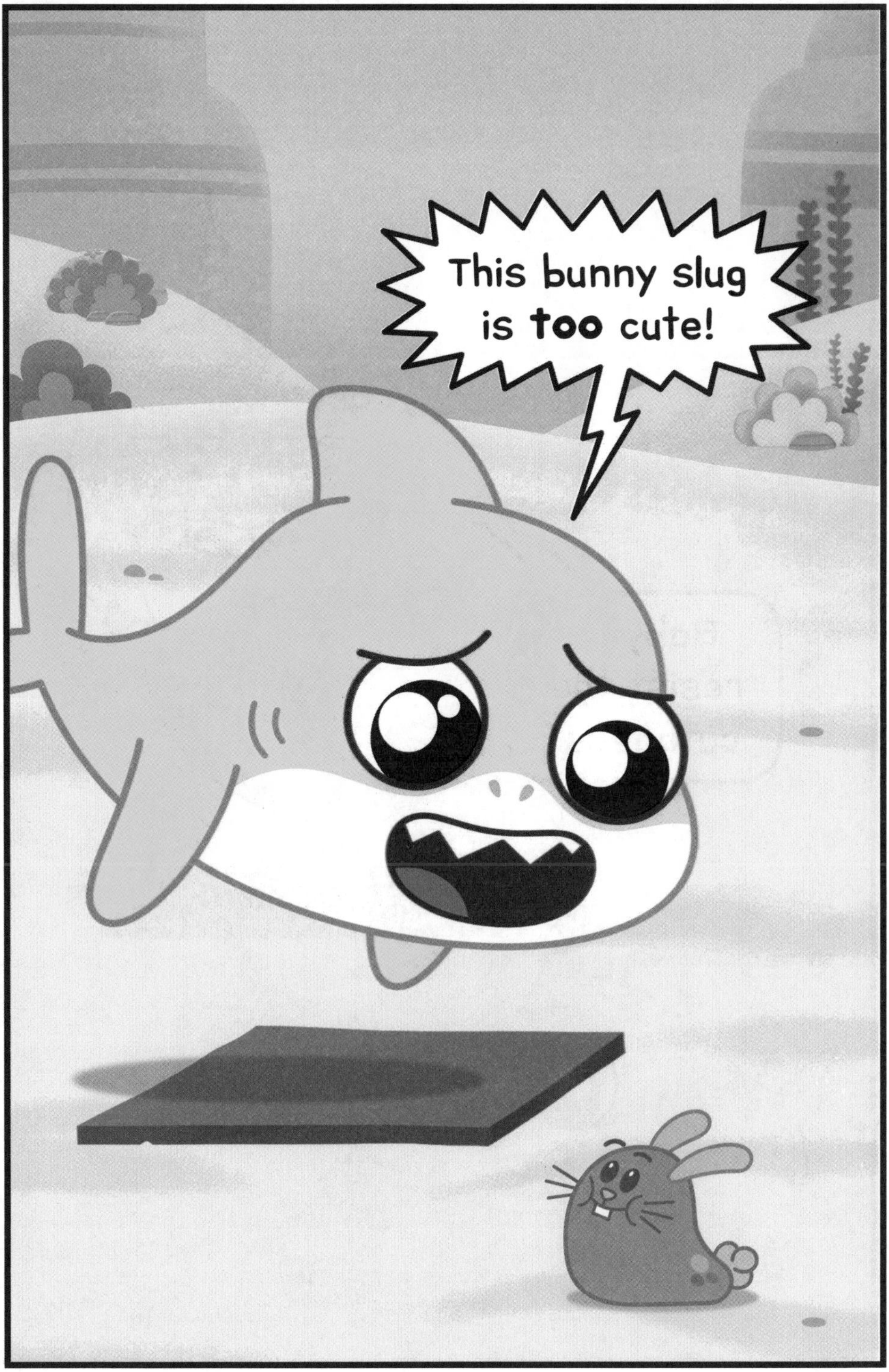
This bunny slug is **too** cute!

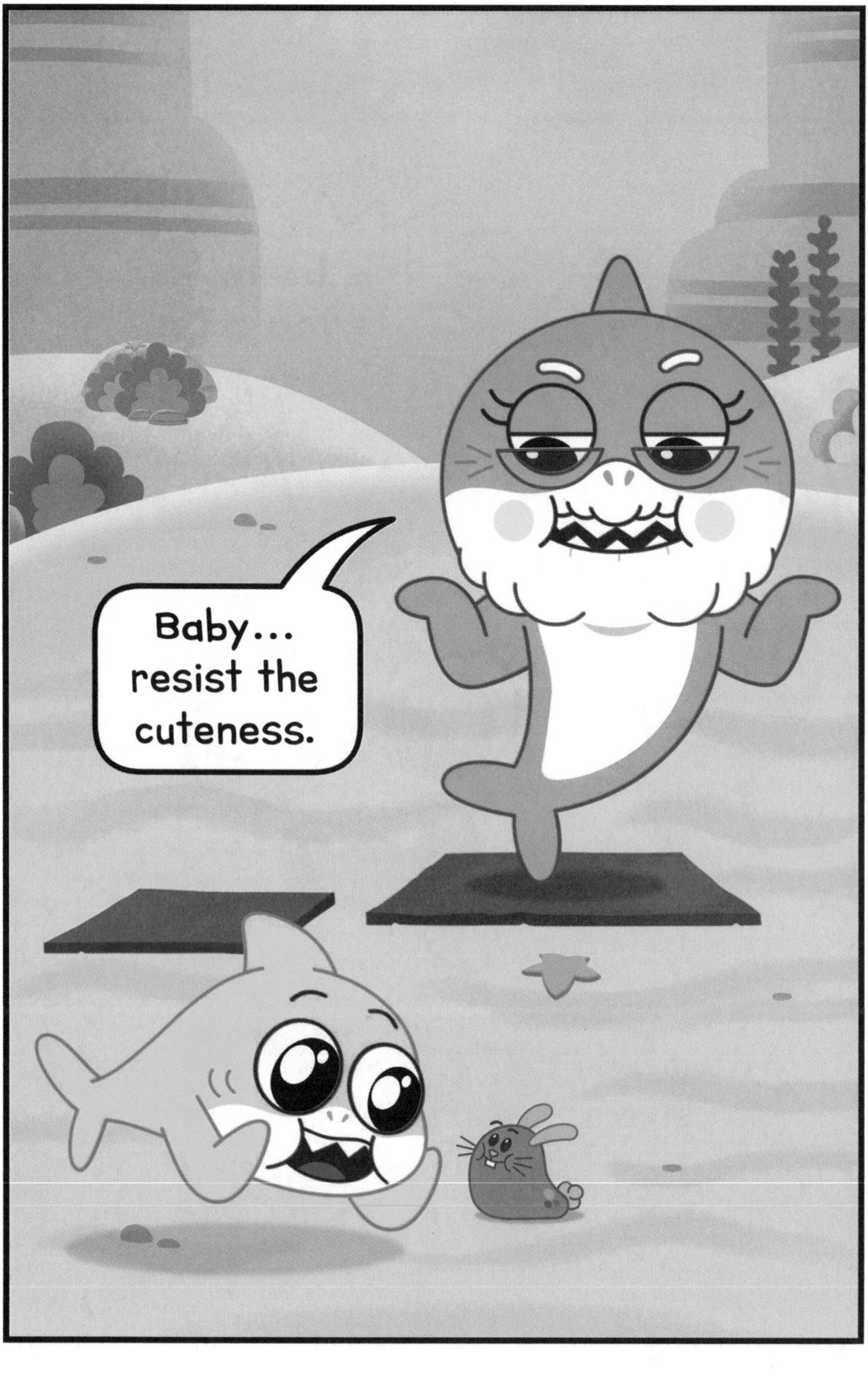
Baby... resist the cuteness.

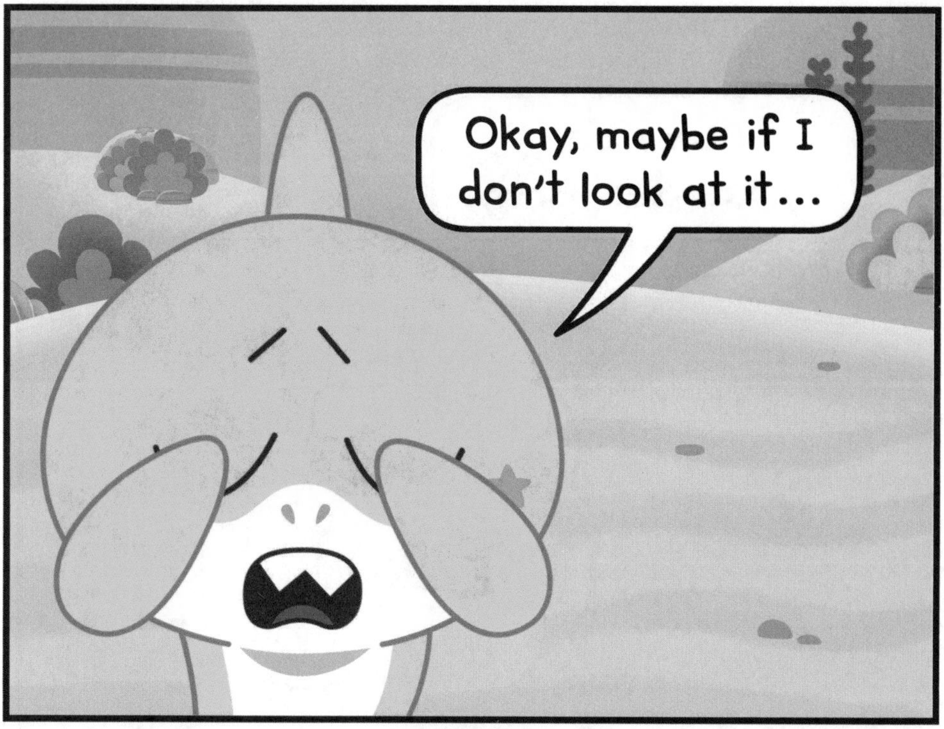
Okay, maybe if I don't look at it...

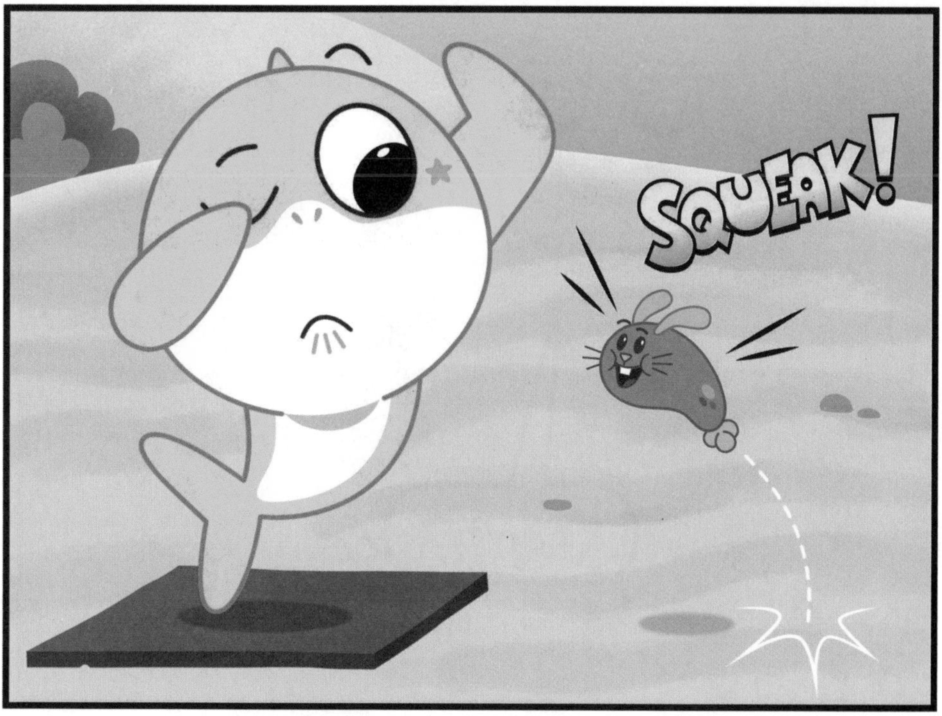
SQUEAK!

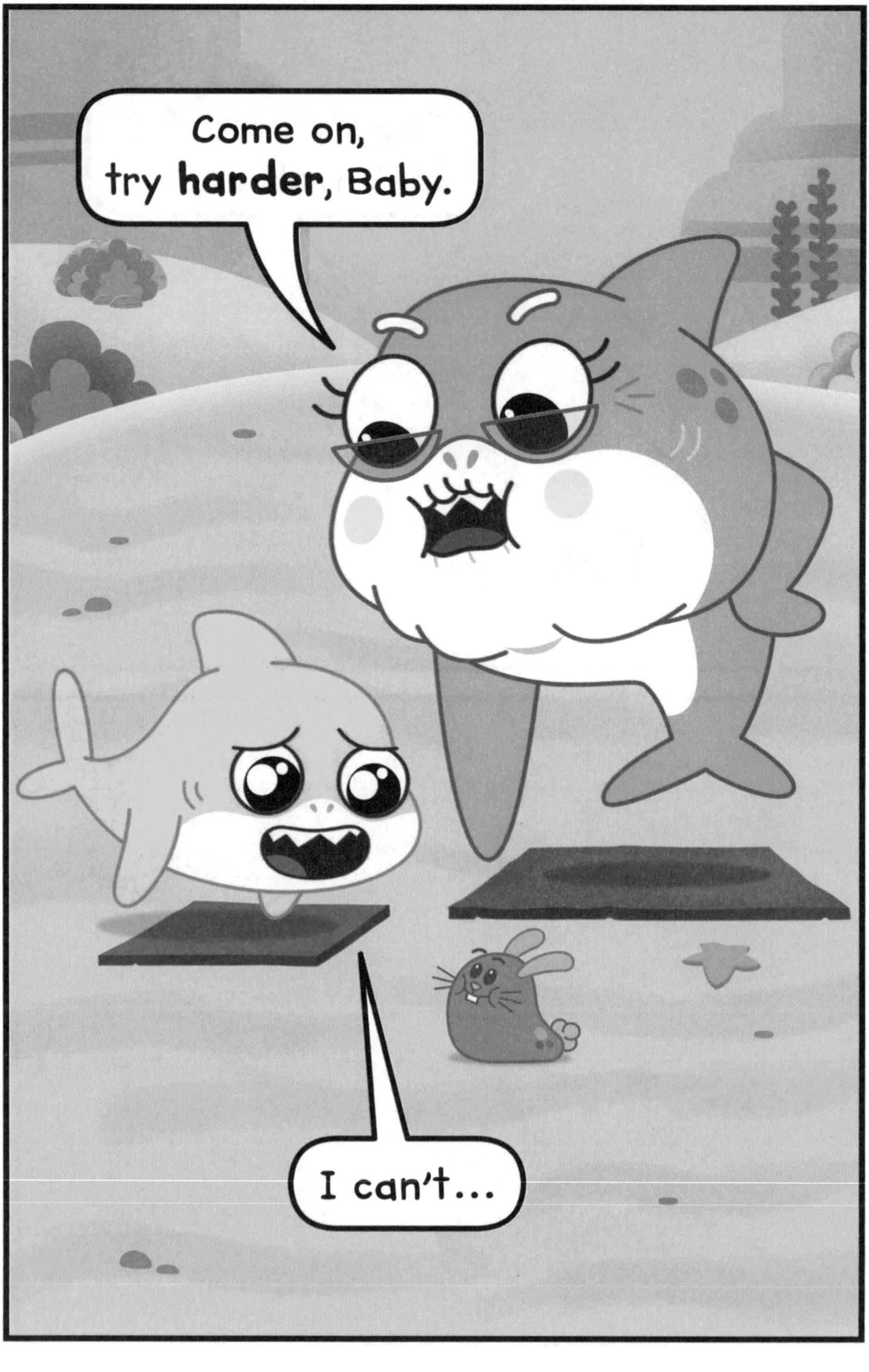
Come on, try **harder**, Baby.
I can't...

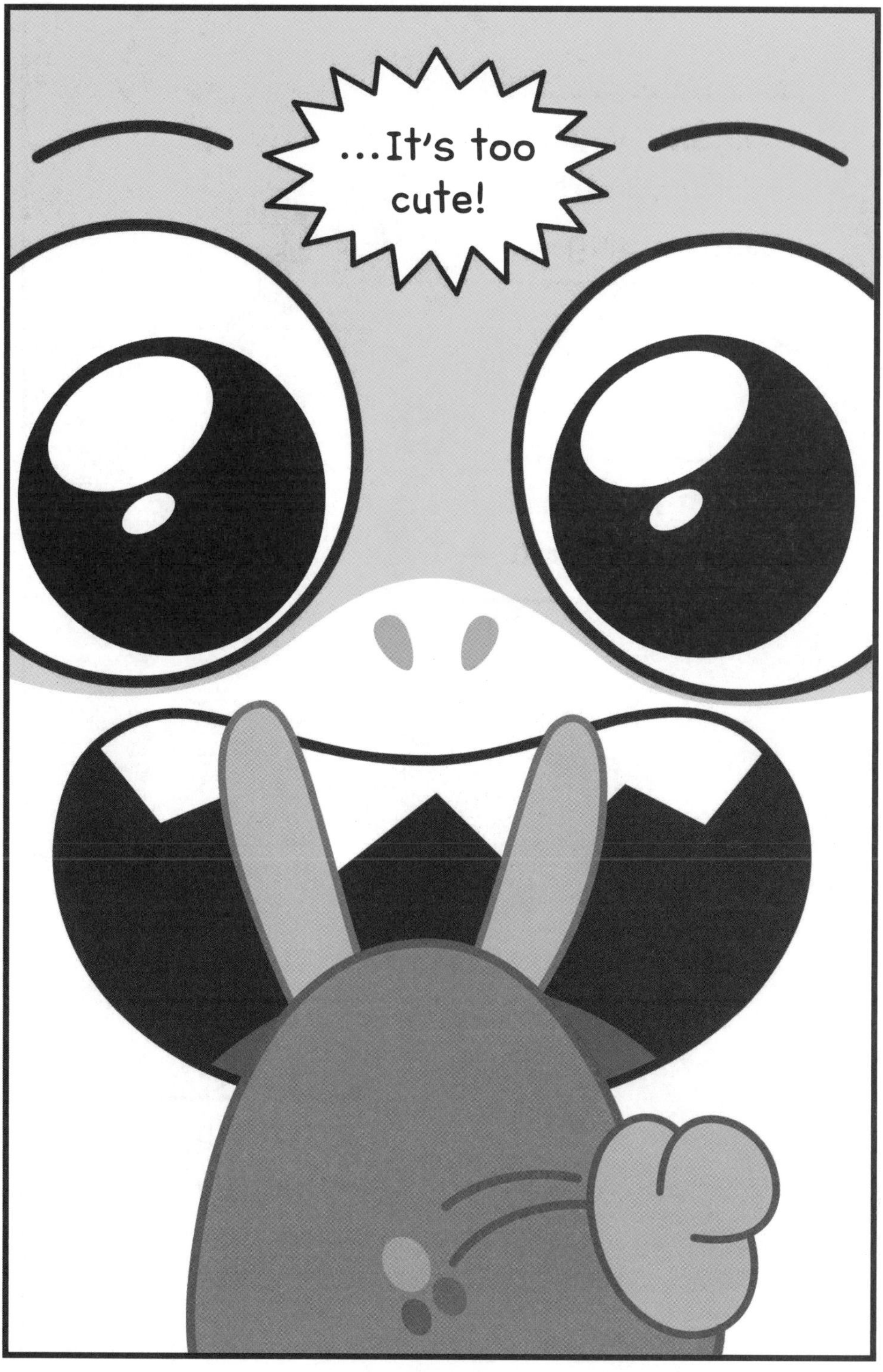
...It's too cute!

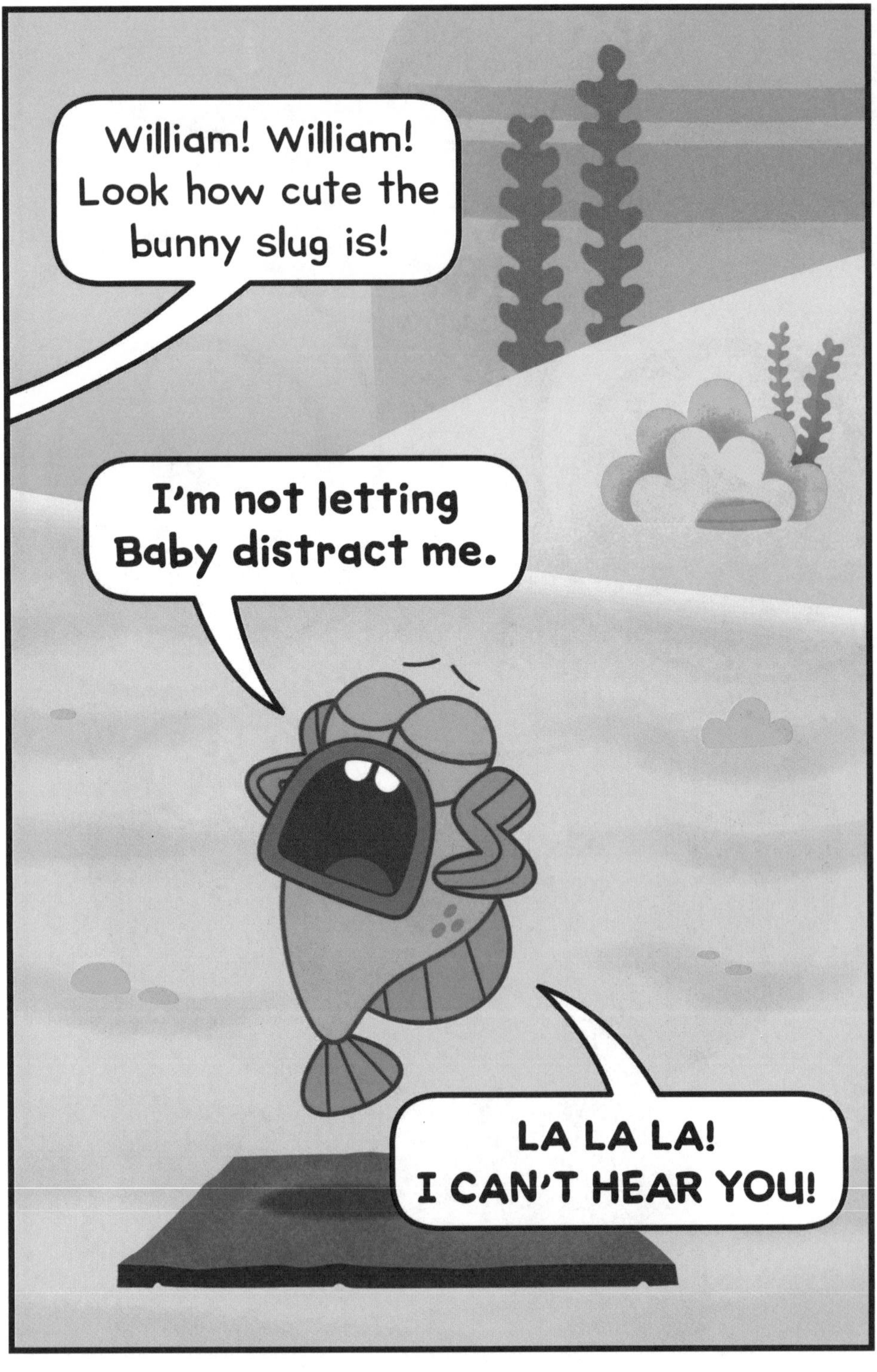
William! William! Look how cute the bunny slug is!
I'm not letting Baby distract me.
LA LA LA! I CAN'T HEAR YOU!

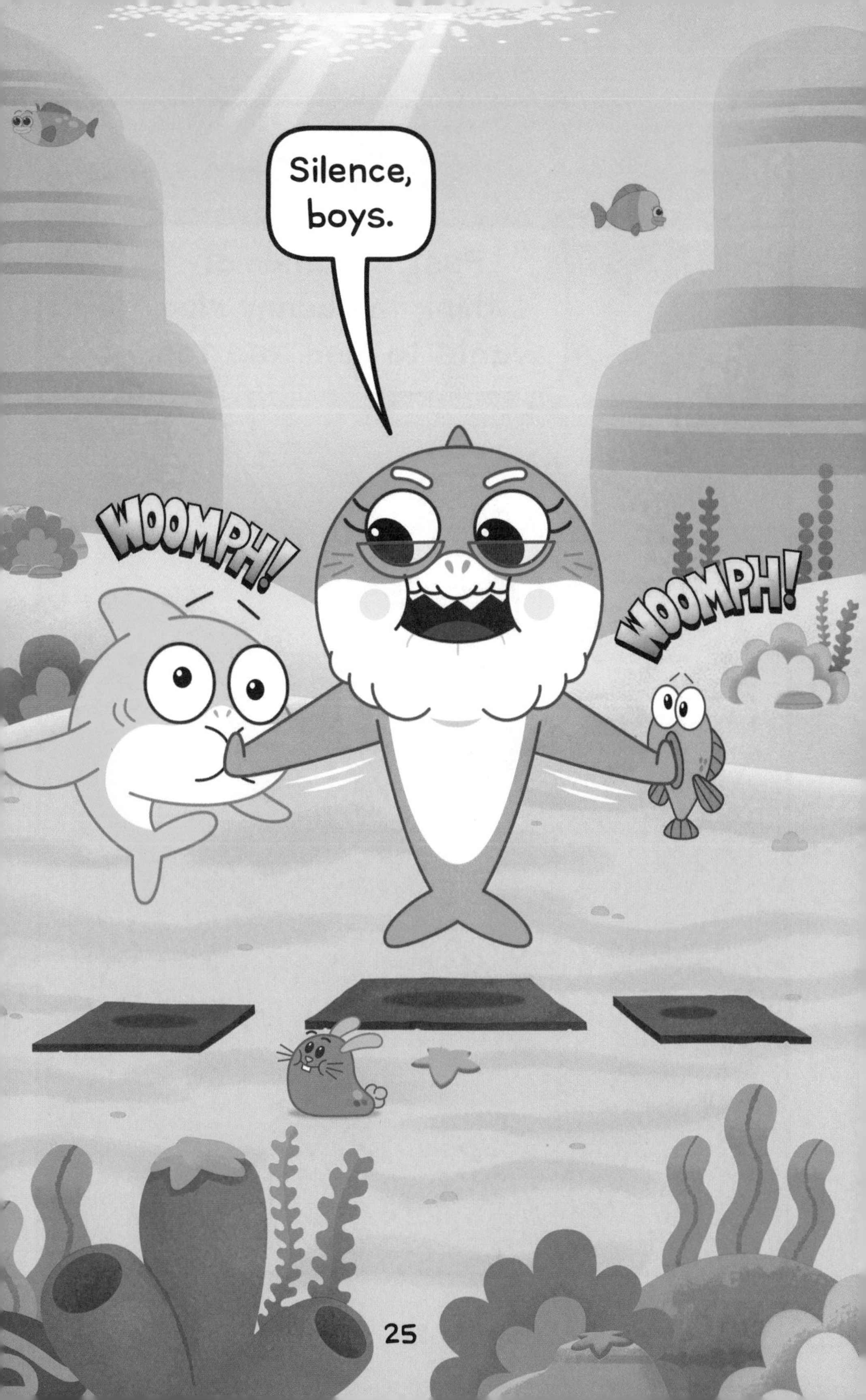
Silence, boys.
WOOMPH!
WOOMPH!

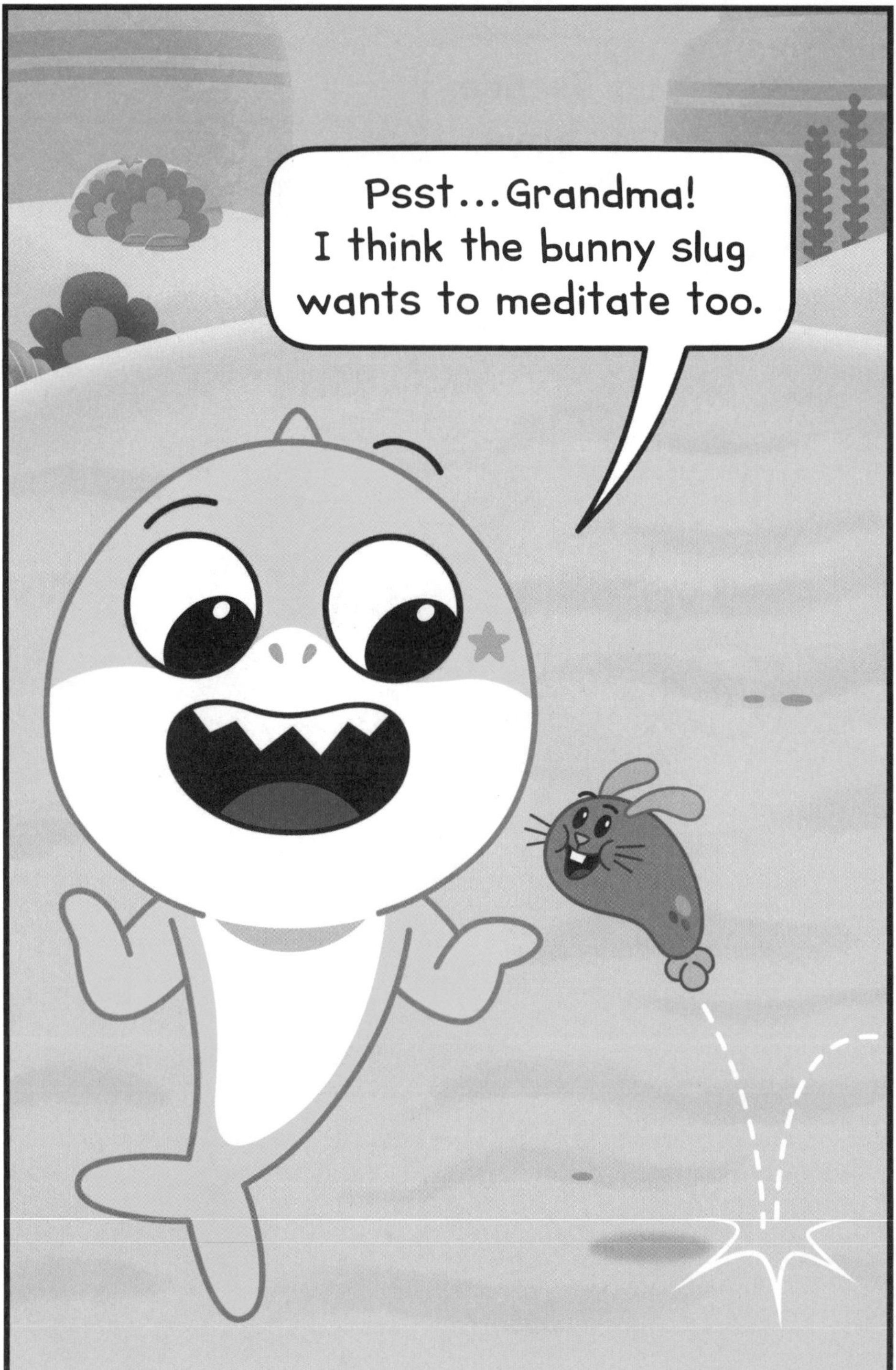
Psst...Grandma!
I think the bunny slug
wants to meditate too.

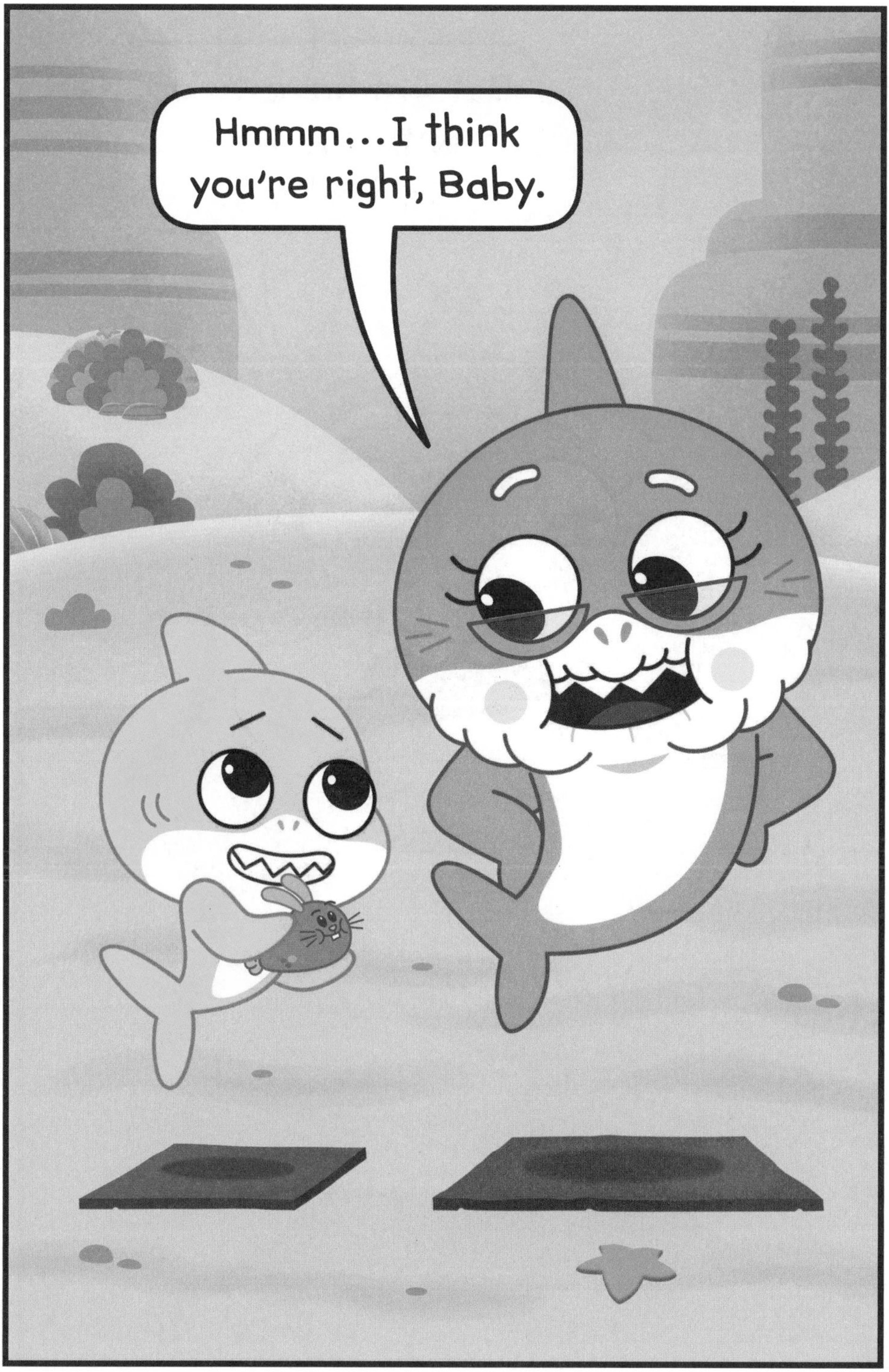
Hmmm...I think you're right, Baby.

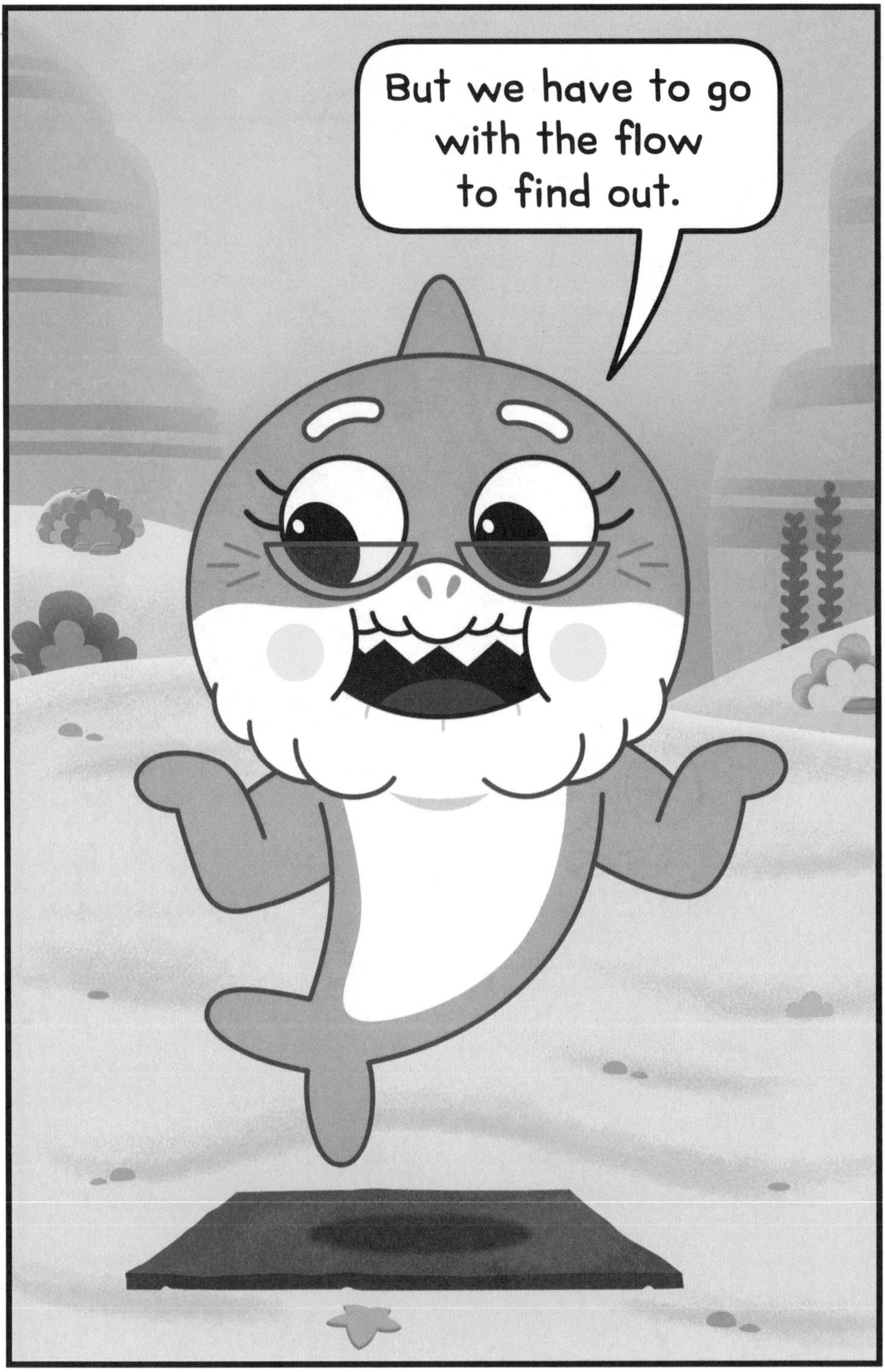
But we have to go with the flow to find out.

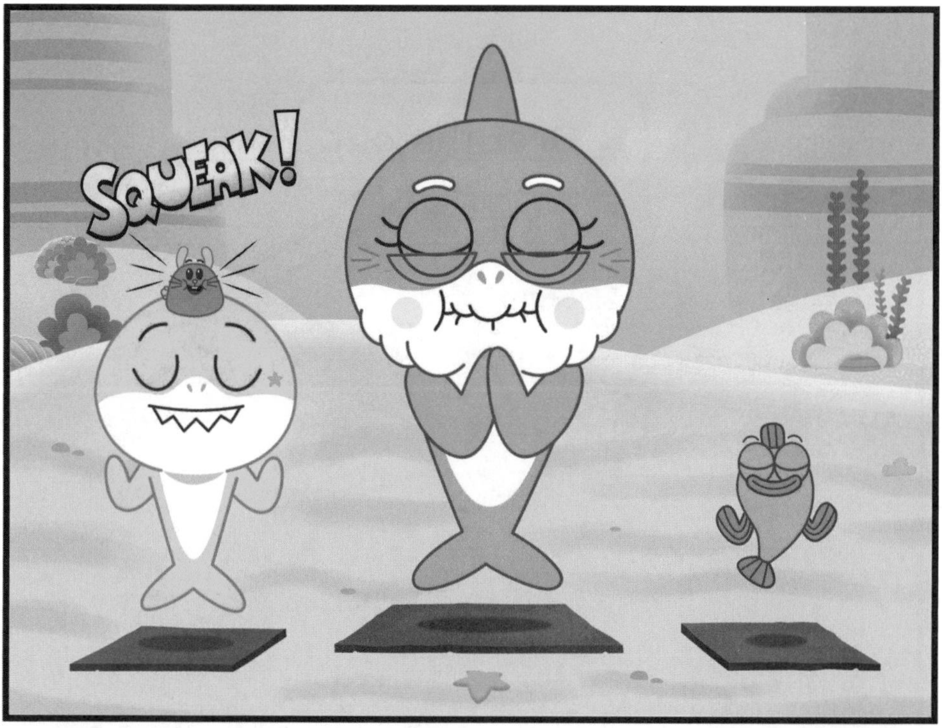
SQUEAK!

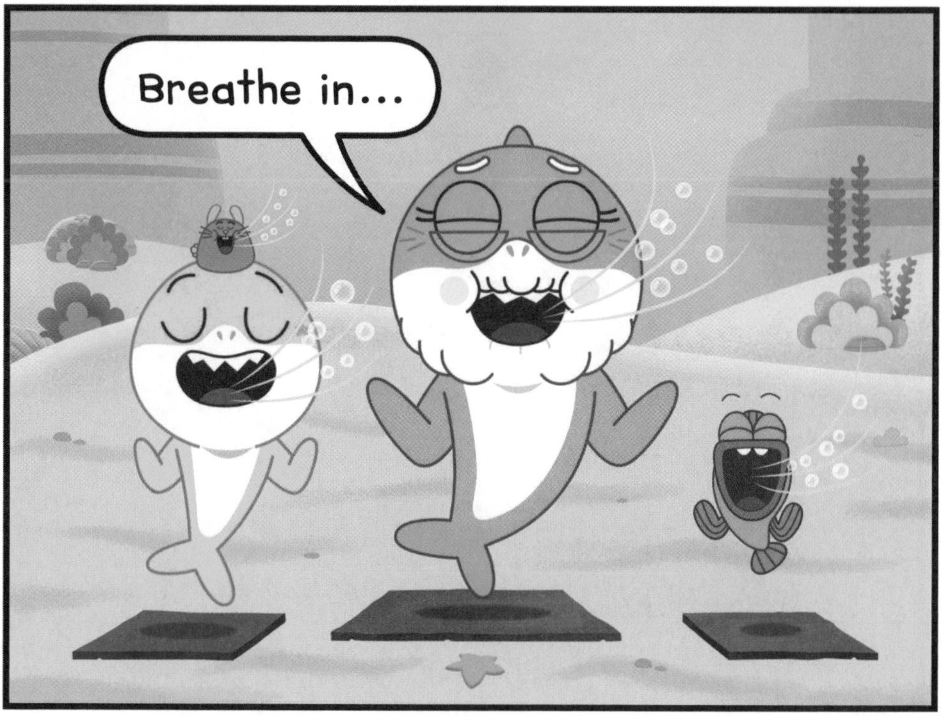
Breathe in...

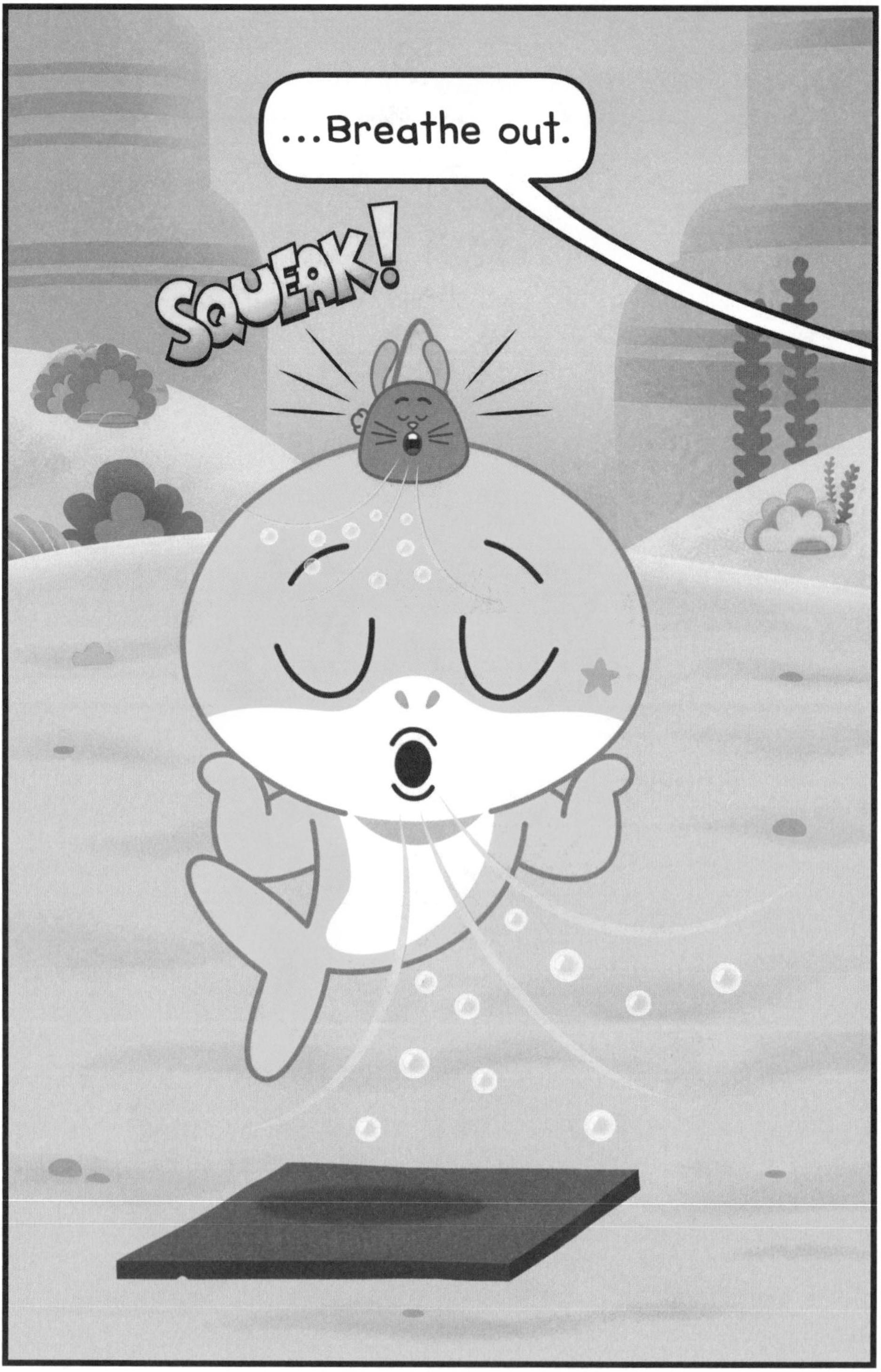
...Breathe out.
SQUEAK!

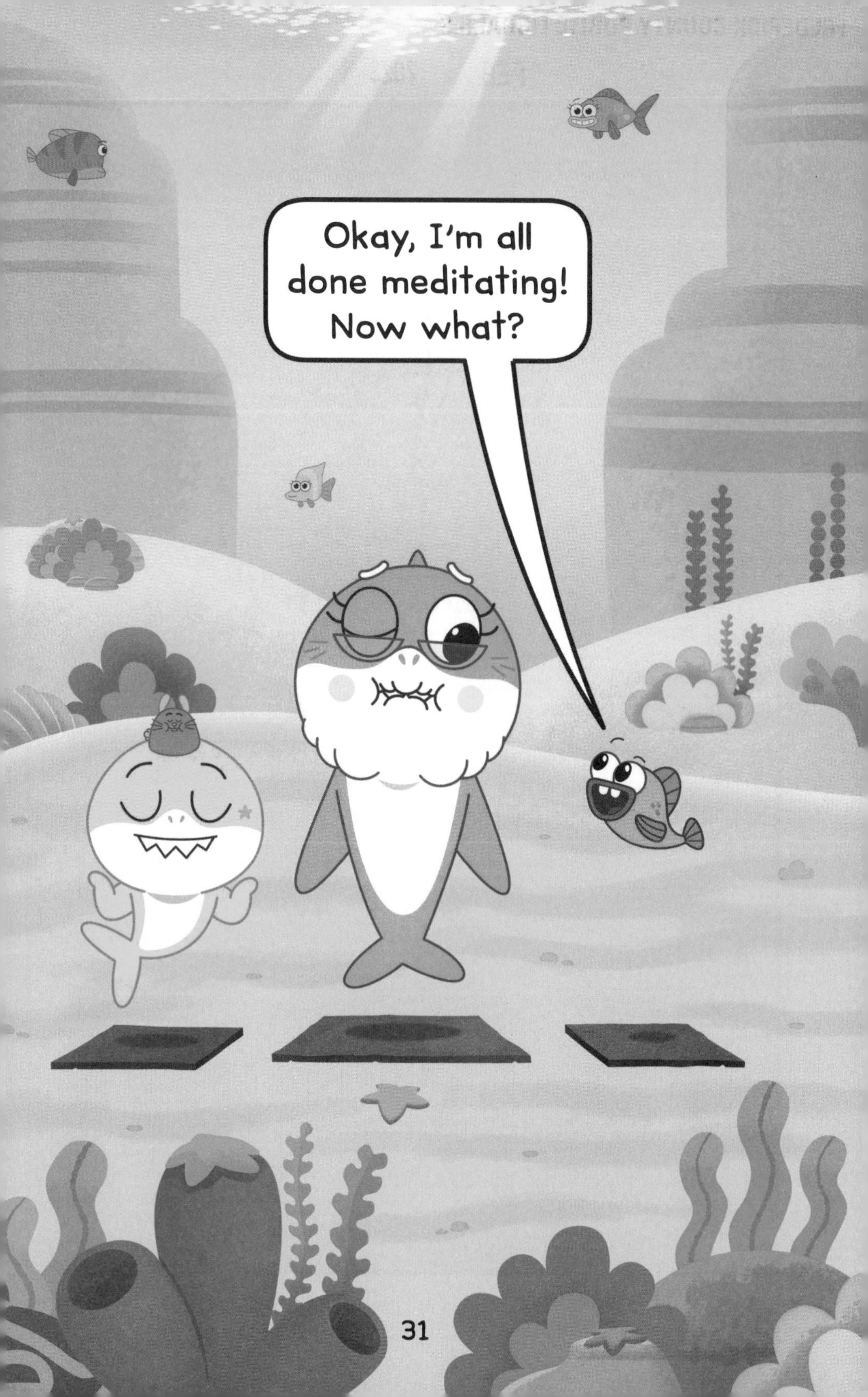
Okay, I'm all done meditating! Now what?

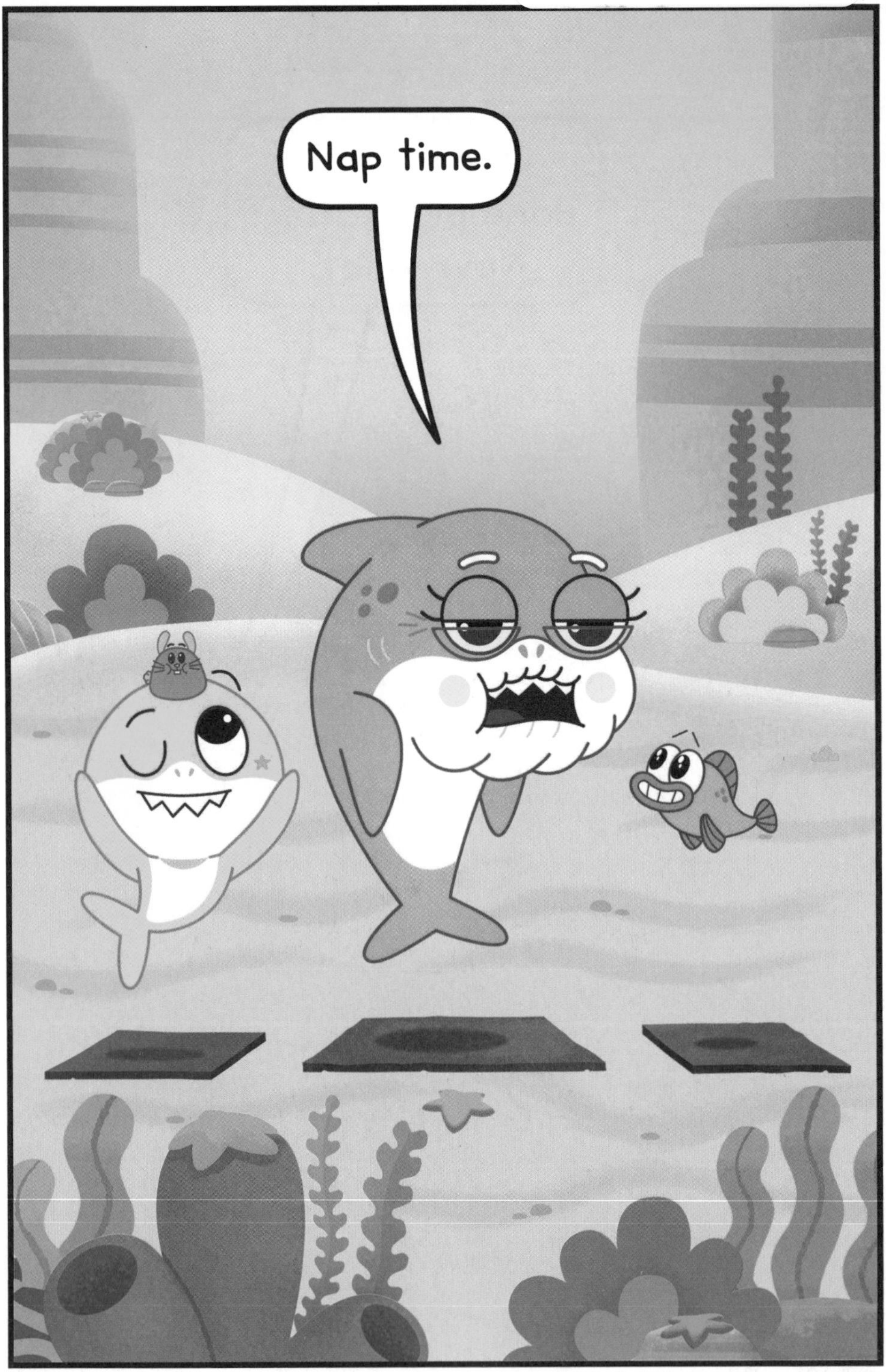
Nap time.